The Christmas Wish

A HOLLY FALLS CHRISTMAS

JUDY POWERS

TOC

PROLOGUE:
The Great Escape

D awn's phone buzzed at an un-Godley hour, which should have been her first clue that the universe was about to implode.

She was sprawled on the narrow couch in the Austin hostel room she shared with Maya, who was currently applying some sort of mystical face serum with the serenity of a Buddhist monk. Maya believed in skincare routines the way other people believed in religion, with absolute faith and a lot of expensive rituals.

The text was from Bartholomew: *Morning! Last night was lovely. I was just ordering a new shower curtain, mine needs replacing. Did you prefer the paisley or the small geometric print? And have you ever had a designated spice drawer?*

Dawn stared at the screen until the words stopped making sense and began to look like hieroglyphs of impending doom, together with the thumbnail pictures of each pattern.

Shower curtain? *Paisley*?

"Maya," she said, "hypothetically speaking, what does it mean when someone asks you about shower curtain patterns?"

Maya didn't open her eyes. "Hypothetically? It means they're nesting. And you're about to bolt like a startled deer."

Dawn's stomach dropped. "I don't bolt."

"You bolted from Portland when Trevor mentioned getting a plant together. You bolted from Seattle when David suggested splitting a Costco membership. You once bolted from a coffee date because the guy mentioned his five-year plan."

"That five-year plan included a joint savings account and named children, Maya. *Named* children. He had a spreadsheet."

"And now Bartholomew wants to discuss home décor." Maya finally opened one eye, which was somehow more judgmental than both eyes would have been. "So what are you going to do?"

Dawn looked back at her phone. *Have you ever had a designated spice drawer?*

A designated spice drawer wasn't organized. It was a declaration of intent. It was saying *we live here together*, and we plan meals together, and *we've reached the stage where we coordinate our seasonings*. Next week, he'd want matching coffee mugs. Then joint bank accounts. Then, burial plots with complementary headstones.

"I need to pack," Dawn said, already moving toward her battered suitcase.

"Of course you do." Maya returned to her serum application. "Where are we fleeing to this time? Please tell me somewhere with decent Wi-Fi. I have a client call tomorrow."

"We?"

"Dawn. Darling. You're about to have a complete meltdown over someone's organizational skills. I'm not leaving you alone with sharp objects and your own overthinking brain."

Dawn started throwing things into her suitcase: the ski boot from Colorado, a Halloween wig she'd forgotten to return, three mismatched shoes because apparently panic made her forget how feet worked. "I'm not having a meltdown. I'm making a strategic exit."

"From what? A man who wants to alphabetize his cumin?"

"From—" Dawn's hands stilled over her suitcase. "From the fact that he's thinking about *our* spice drawer. Our shower curtain. Like we're a unit. Like we're permanent."

Maya sat up, abandoning her skincare ritual entirely, which was how Dawn knew this was serious. "And that terrifies you because...?"

"Because I don't *do* permanent. I told him that from the very start!" The words came out sharper than she'd intended. "I do temporary. I do fun while it lasts. I do great while we're both free to leave whenever we want. I don't do spice drawers and shower curtains and whatever comes after that."

"What comes after that?"

Dawn's suitcase chose that moment to burst open with a sound like a dying accordion, scattering her personal underwear across the hostel floor.

"That," she said, staring at the chaos. "That's what comes after. Everything falls apart, and then you're stuck cleaning up the mess with someone who's seen you at your worst and decides they'd rather organize spices alone."

Maya was quiet for a long moment, watching Dawn scramble to repack her exploded life. "You know that's not how it works, right? Sometimes people stick around because they've seen you at your worst and decide they'd rather reorganize spice drawers together."

Dawn's chest did something complicated and painful. "I can't risk it."

"So where are you running to this time?"

Dawn's phone was already open to flight apps, her fingers moving with the practiced efficiency of someone who'd turned fleeing into an art form. "Home. Holly Falls, Indiana."

"Home? You rarely ever go home."

"It's the only place I can afford on short notice." Dawn held her suitcase closed with one hand while she used the pink silk scarf Maya had abandoned in Seattle to tie it shut. "Besides, it's almost Christmas. Family emergency."

"What's the emergency?"

"Spending the holidays pretending I have my life together while my mother asks why I'm still single and my sister gives me that look that says she knows exactly why I'm really there."

Maya sighed and started packing her own bag. "Well, this should be interesting."

"You don't have to come with me."

"Are you kidding? I wouldn't miss this train wreck for anything. Besides," Maya grinned, "I've never seen you run toward something you can't actually outrun."

Dawn's phone buzzed again. Another text from Bartholomew: *I don't understand. Did I do something wrong?*

Dawn stared at it, her thumb hovering over the keyboard. How did you explain that a spice drawer felt like a cage? Those shower curtain consultations looked like the first step toward joint tax returns and shared burial plots?

She sent a quick text: *I can't do this,* then blocked his number, which made her feel like a monster and a coward, and exactly the kind of person who deserved to spend Christmas explaining herself to her disappointed family.

"Come on," Maya said, shouldering her perfectly organized travel bag. "Let's go watch you have a breakdown in your hometown. This is going to be better than reality TV."

Twenty minutes later, they were in an Uber to Austin-Bergstrom International, Dawn's suitcase held together with determination and Maya's silk scarf. The driver kept trying to make conversation about the beautiful morning while Dawn frantically searched for flights.

"Holly Falls, Indiana," she told Maya, showing her the only affordable option. "Population 8,000. Home to the most aggressively festive Christmas celebration this side of Hallmark, and the last place on earth I want to spend the next three weeks."

"Perfect," Maya said cheerfully. "What could go wrong?"

***

The airport was a special kind of purgatory at dawn, too bright, too empty, filled with the kind of people who had their lives together enough to catch 8 AM flights. Dawn and Maya were decidedly not those people.

"Holly Falls, Indiana," Dawn told the ticket counter agent, who looked at them with the practiced sympathy of someone who'd seen many a pre-dawn breakdown. "Two tickets. One way."

"Two one-way tickets to Holly Falls is $494 total. I can get you there with one connection through Indianapolis. I have seats 42C and 42D available."

"Both window and middle?" Dawn's heart sank.

"I'm afraid the flight's quite full. Will that be all right?"

No. Window seats were traps. Trapped against the fuselage for three hours with no escape route and nothing to look at but clouds shaped like future regrets. But Maya was already pulling out her credit card, because

Maya was the kind of person who solved problems instead of spiraling about airplane seating metaphors.

The airline's automated confirmation message was unnaturally cheerful: "Your flights to Holly Falls are confirmed. Departure 6:45 AM, gate B12. We know you have a choice in airlines, and we're glad you chose us for your journey home."

Home. The word sat wrong in Dawn's chest.

Security was its own nightmare. Dawn's hastily packed suitcase triggered every possible alarm. The TSA agent unpacked it with the grim efficiency of an archaeologist uncovering evidence of poor life choices: the ski boot, the Halloween wig, three mismatched shoes, and, mortifyingly, the can of Cream of Mushroom soup, which rolled across the floor with a sound like a judgment bell.

"Ma'am, you can't bring soup through security," the agent said with the patience of someone who'd seen it all.

"I didn't... I don't even like mushroom soup." Dawn scrambled after the runaway can. "I was packing in a panic. There was a spice drawer situation."

The agent's expression suggested this explanation raised more questions than it answered.

"Family emergency," Maya added, producing her own perfectly organized carry-on for inspection. "She's fleeing domestic organization."

The agent's expression didn't change much.

Twenty minutes later, they were finally through security, Dawn's dignity in tatters and her suitcase somehow even more chaotic than before. Maya steered her toward their gate with the gentle firmness of a prison warden.

At the gate, Dawn stared at their boarding passes with mounting dread. "Window seat. Of course. Trapped against the fuselage for three hours with no escape."

Maya glanced at her own ticket. "I've got the middle. Want to trade? I don't mind windows."

"You'd do that?"

"Dawn, you're having a major crisis over spice organization. The least I can do is save you from airplane-induced claustrophobia." Maya held out her boarding pass. "Besides, I like looking at clouds. They don't judge my life choices."

Dawn nearly cried with relief. "You're the best terrible influence I've ever had."

"I prefer 'enabler with excellent skincare,'" Maya said, settling into an uncomfortable airport chair. "Now, while we wait to board this escape pod to your past, want to tell me about Holly Falls? Because something tells me there's more to this story than Christmas trees and family obligations."

Dawn's throat tightened. "Holly Falls. The only place I could run to, even though running there meant running into Jack. Into the memory of the last time I'd almost stayed."

Maya raised an eyebrow. "Jack?"

"Single dad. Firefighter. His daughter Lily is five and perfect and calls me 'Dawn-Dawn' like we're family." Dawn's chest did that complicated thing again. "Two years ago, I almost didn't leave. I almost stayed for Christmas. Almost let myself think maybe I could build something permanent."

"What happened?"

"I woke up on New Year's Day on his couch, watching him make pancakes for Lily, and realized I was playing house. Really, truly playing house, with a man who deserved someone who wouldn't bolt the second things felt too real." Dawn stared out the terminal windows at the planes preparing for takeoff. "So I bolted."

"Before breakfast?"

"No, after breakfast. I left a note explaining why, and told him I had a work emergency and caught the first flight out." Dawn's voice went quiet. "Jack didn't try to stop me; he said that Lily cried."

Maya was quiet for a long moment. "And now you're going back."

"Now I'm going back to spend three weeks pretending I have my life together while my mother asks pointed questions about grandchildren and my sister gives me that look that says she knows exactly why I'm really there."

"Flight 447 to Indianapolis, now boarding group one," the gate agent announced with airline-mandated cheer.

Maya stood, shouldering her perfectly organized travel bag. "Come on. Time to face the music. Or at least the Christmas carols."

The flight to Indianapolis was turbulent. Not the plane, the plane was fine. But Dawn was wedged between a guy who was constantly laughing at YouTube videos on his phone, and a woman who was knitting what appeared to be a Christmas sweater for someone she clearly loved very much.

Dawn tried to read, tried to sleep, tried not to think about Bartholomew.

The Indianapolis connection was brief, just enough time to grab coffee and question all her life choices in a generic airport terminal. The commuter plane to Holly Falls was smaller and fuller, with people who looked like they were going home for the holidays.

They settled into their seats, Maya by the window, Dawn in the middle, both of them wedged against a businessman who immediately fell asleep and started snoring. Dawn tried to read, tried to sleep, tried not to think about Jack's face when he'd found her note, or the way Lily had asked Amy where Dawn-Dawn had gone.

It wasn't until they were descending toward Holly Falls that Dawn pressed her face to the window past Maya, watching the landscape unfold below them.

Snow-dusted rooftops. The town square, with its gazebo already outlined in Christmas lights. Main Street with its row of cheerful storefronts. And there, in the center of it all, the enormous Christmas tree that would be going up any day now.

Her stomach dropped, not from turbulence. From the feeling that she might be running toward something she couldn't outrun. Something that looked suspiciously like home.

"You okay?" Maya asked, following her gaze.

Dawn pressed her forehead against the cool window. "Ask me in three weeks."

The plane touched down with a gentle bump, and Dawn's phone immediately buzzed with a text from Amy: *Remember that I have your phone tracked? Saw you're coming home. Everything okay?*

Dawn stared at the message, her thumb hovering over the keyboard. How did you explain that you were fleeing spice drawer commitment while running toward the man whose pancakes had once made you want to stay forever?

Everything's fine, she typed back. *Just felt like spending Christmas with the family.*

Three dots appeared immediately. Then: *That's exactly what someone with a family emergency would say. I'll have wine ready.*

Despite everything, the spice drawer, the blocked number, the fact that she was about to spend three weeks in the same town as the man she'd run from, Dawn smiled.

"Welcome to Holly Falls," Maya said, peering out the window at the small terminal building decorated with enough garland to supply a forest. "This should be interesting."

Dawn gathered her disaster of a carry-on, her heart doing something between panic and anticipation. "You have no idea."

Chapter 1:
Welcome Home

The rental car counter at Holly Falls Terminal looked like it had been designed by someone who'd given up on life but still believed in aggressive cheerfulness. Dawn stood in line behind a businessman arguing about GPS upgrades while Maya scrolled through hotel options on her phone.

"Holly Falls Inn looks charming," Maya said, showing Dawn a photo of a Victorian building that looked like it had been dipped in Christmas frosting. "Three stars, continental breakfast, and—this is important—cable TV for when I need to escape whatever family drama you're about to unleash."

"You could stay at my parents' house. There's a guest room."

Maya gave her the look she reserved for truly terrible ideas. "Dawn. Darling. I love you, but I'm not sleeping under the same roof as people who are going to spend the next three weeks psychoanalyzing your commitment issues. I need somewhere to retreat when you inevitably have a breakdown over Christmas cookies."

Fair point.

Dawn stepped up to the counter, credit card already in hand. "I need a car for about three weeks. Something with good tires and reliable heat."

"And GPS," the agent added helpfully. "First time in Indiana?"

"No, I grew up here. I just like having my own transportation."

The agent's expression suggested this was either very sensible or mildly suspicious. Dawn didn't clarify that having her own car meant having her own exit strategy. That rental cars were freedom machines disguised as economy sedans. That the ability to leave at any moment was the only thing standing between her and a complete nervous breakdown in her mother's aggressively festive living room.

"The Corolla is our most popular model," the agent said. "Excellent gas mileage, reliable in snow."

"Perfect."

Twenty minutes later, Dawn was following Maya's Uber through the familiar countryside toward Holly Falls, her hands white-knuckled on the steering wheel despite having driven this route a hundred times. The landscape rolled past in shades of brown and gray, fields stubbled with the remnants of corn harvest, farmhouses tucked between bare trees.

And then Holly Falls appeared around a bend in the road, and Dawn's chest did that complicated thing it always did when she saw home.

Someone had been busy. Thanksgiving was still two days away, but the town was already dressed for Christmas like an overenthusiastic teenager going to prom. Garland wrapped every lamppost on Main Street. The gazebo in the town square wore a crown of white lights. Store windows glowed with red and green displays that were both charming and aggressive in their festivity.

It was beautiful. It was ridiculous. It was exactly the kind of small-town Christmas-card perfection that made Dawn feel suffocated and homesick at the same time.

She pulled into the driveway of her childhood home and right away understood why her chest felt tight. Her mother had clearly been decorating since Labor Day. The Victorian house—already imposing with its gabled roof and wraparound porch—now looked like it had been attacked by a Christmas fairy with impulse control issues. Garland. Wreaths. White lights outline every architectural detail. An inflatable snowman on the front lawn that was either waving its arm or surrendering to the decorating police.

Dawn sat in the car for a moment, engine running, escape route confirmed. Her phone showed three missed calls from Amy and a text: I see you in the driveway. Stop stalling.

Sometimes having a twin was like living with a very organized stalker.

She turned off the car, grabbed her disaster of a suitcase, and steeled herself for impact.

The front door opened before she reached it, a family tradition that never failed to make her feel like she was walking into a gentle ambush. Her mother, Patricia, appeared in the doorway wearing the kind of apron that suggested she'd been baking since dawn and intended to continue until New Year's.

"Dawn Elizabeth Donovan." Patricia pulled her into a hug that smelled like apples and cinnamon and home. "You look thin. Are you eating? That jacket isn't warm enough. Indiana winter will kill you if you're not careful."

"Hi, Mom. I'm fine. The jacket's fine. I've survived Indiana winters before."

"Not recently. You've been gallivanting around warmer climates, building up no tolerance for real weather." Patricia steered her inside with the gentle efficiency of someone who'd perfected the art of maternal management. "Doug! She's here!"

The house smelled like pine and nutmeg and felt like the specific anxiety that came from hosting holidays. Every surface that could hold a decoration was holding three. The Christmas tree, a towering monument to holiday excess, dominated the corner of the living room, already fully decorated despite Thanksgiving being two days away.

Her father emerged from behind the tree, wrestling with a strand of lights that appeared to be winning. Doug Donovan was the kind of man who approached Christmas decorating like military strategy, methodical, thorough, and occasionally defeated by superior forces.

"Dawn!" He held up one hand, which was tangled in blinking lights. "Good to see you. Can you help me with... no, never mind, I've got it. How was the flight?"

"Turbulent. Literally and metaphysically."

"That's my girl. Always making everything philosophical." He grinned, the lights choosing that moment to cooperate and untangle. "Your mother's been cooking since Tuesday. I think we have enough food to feed half the county."

"Just the family," Patricia called from the kitchen. "And maybe a few extras if people stop by. You know how it is during the holidays."

Dawn did know. During Christmas, her mother's house became a gravitational center for every stray soul in Holly Falls. People "stopped by" for coffee and stayed for dinner. Neighbors appeared with casseroles and disappeared with containers of Patricia's famous cookies. The house became a Christmas waystation for anyone who needed feeding, warming, or general maternal care.

It was overwhelming. It was wonderful. It was the kind of permanent, rooted, committed lifestyle that made Dawn's skin crawl.

"Dawn-Dawn!"

Dawn turned just as Amy emerged from the kitchen, and the difference between them hit her like it always did: the same face, the same height, the same brown eyes, but everything else was the opposite. Where Dawn was

18

rumpled from travel and stress, Amy was pressed and put-together. Where Dawn's hair escaped from its ponytail in rebellious waves, Amy's fell in a neat bob that never seemed to move. Where Dawn wore paint-stained jeans and a vintage jacket, Amy wore a crisp sweater and an apron that somehow made her look more professional instead of domestic.

Amy was also holding a clipboard with color-coded tabs, which was either very Amy or a sign that the apocalypse was imminent.

"You look terrible," Amy said, pulling her into a hug. "Travel anxiety or life anxiety?"

"Both. Multiple types. I'm an anxiety sampler platter."

"I can work with that. Come on, Mom made coffee that's proven to be liquid comfort food."

They migrated to the kitchen, where Patricia had laid out enough food to sustain a small army through a siege. Cookies, cake, three kinds of bread, and something that smelled like it had been cooked during the Carter administration—fruit cake, blech.

Dawn perched on the kitchen counter near the window, old habit, proximity to an escape route, while Amy settled into a chair at the kitchen table like a person who belonged somewhere. The contrast wasn't lost on her. Amy belonged. Dawn visited.

"So," Amy said, consulting her clipboard with the casual efficiency of someone running a small corporation, "I need you to volunteer."

Dawn nearly choked on her coffee. "I've been here four minutes."

"Four and a half. I was timing it." Amy made a note on her clipboard. "The Christmas festival needs help, and you're here for three weeks with no concrete plans and a pathological need to stay busy when you're avoiding dealing with your feelings."

"I don't avoid—"

"Dawn. You once organized a photography exhibition in Portland to avoid thinking about whether you actually liked the guy you were dating."

Fair point.

"What kind of volunteering?" Dawn asked, which was a mistake, but Amy had perfected the art of cornering people when they were caffeinated and vulnerable.

"Festival setup. Planning. General organization." Amy's clipboard somehow managed to look official and threatening at the same time. "There's a new volunteer helping with the logistics. Very enthusiastic about Christmas. Very helpful. Very good at managing complicated projects."

Something in Amy's tone suggested she had opinions about this new volunteer. Amy always had opinions, but she usually shared them right away and in great detail. Mysterious Amy was unsettling.

"I don't know," Dawn said, edging closer to the window. "I was thinking more along the lines of helping Mom with cooking. Low-key. Domestic. No long-term commitments."

"The festival is one month, Dawn. That's hardly a lifetime commitment."

"One month is four weeks. Four weeks is basically a season. A season is a quarter of a year. Before you know it, you're signing leases and discussing joint bank accounts and someone's organizing your spice drawer."

Amy and Patricia exchanged one of those looks that siblings and mothers perfected, the kind that said she's doing it again without using actual words.

"It's Christmas festival volunteering, not a marriage proposal," Amy said.

"That's how it starts. Small commitments. Then bigger commitments. Then you wake up one morning and someone's replaced all your travel mugs with matching dinnerware and you're discussing the pros and cons of different cable packages."

"Dawn," Patricia said, settling into the chair across from Amy with her own cup of coffee. "Honey. Are you seeing someone?"

Dawn choked on her coffee. Actually choked. the kind of choking that required back-patting and concerned maternal hovering. "No," she managed between coughs. "Definitely not. Absolutely not seeing anyone."

"But you were seeing someone," Amy observed, which was why having a twin sister was like living with a detective who shared your DNA and knew all your tells.

"I was seeing someone. Past tense. Very past tense. Ancient history past tense."

"What happened?"

Dawn stared into her coffee cup, looking for answers in the foam. "Spice drawer."

Patricia blinked. "I'm sorry?"

"He wanted to organize spices. Together. As a unit. Like a team." Dawn's voice went slightly higher. "He had opinions about shower curtains. Paisley shower curtains. Who has opinions about paisley?"

Amy made a note on her clipboard, probably something like sister having breakdown over home décor. "So you ran."

"I made a strategic exit."

"You ran."

"I relocated. Strategically. With purpose."

"To here. To Holly Falls. The place you always run to when you're running from something." Amy's voice was gentle but pointed, which was Amy's specialty. "Which brings us back to the festival volunteering. Something to do with your hands while you figure out what you're running from."

Doug chose that moment to wander into the kitchen, Christmas lights successfully conquered, looking for coffee and unaware he was walking into family therapy disguised as holiday planning.

"How's the festival coming along?" he asked Amy, settling into the remaining chair and reaching for the plate of cookies. "That new fellow still helping with the setup?"

"Thomas? Yes, he's been incredibly helpful. Very organized. Very good with logistics." Amy's voice went neutral again, which meant she had opinions about Thomas that she wasn't sharing. "He's from out of town, staying at the resort. Very enthusiastic about Holly Falls Christmas traditions."

Dawn wasn't really listening. She was thinking about her unbooked return flight. About the rental car in the driveway. About the fact that she'd fled a spice drawer and landed in a place where Christmas volunteering was apparently a blood sport and her sister had mysterious opinions about helpful out-of-towners.

"Dawn?" Patricia's voice pulled her back to the kitchen. "I asked if you're planning to stay through New Year's."

The question hung in the air like mistletoe, dangerous and unavoidable.

"I haven't booked a return flight yet," Dawn said.

Amy's eyebrows went up. Dawn never left anything unbooked. Dawn planned exits the way other people planned vacations, obsessively, with backup options and contingency plans.

"Well," Patricia said, refilling Dawn's coffee cup with the determination of someone who intended to caffeinate her daughter into staying, "we'll just have to make sure you have plenty to keep you busy. Starting with the Christmas festival."

Dawn looked around the kitchen—at her mother's hopeful expression, at her father's gentle expectation, at Amy's clipboard of organized good intentions. Outside the window, Holly Falls sparkled with aggressive festivity and the promise of three weeks of family dinners and pointed questions about her love life.

She could leave. The rental car was in the driveway. Her suitcase was still technically packed. She could be on a plane by morning, fleeing toward some warm climate where people didn't organize spices or have opinions about shower curtains.

But Maya was right. She was running toward something she couldn't outrun. And maybe, just maybe, it was time to stop running long enough to figure out what that something was.

"Okay," she said, the word surprising her as much as everyone else. "I'll volunteer for the festival."

Amy smiled and made a note on her clipboard. "Perfect. The festival meeting will be as soon as I can arrange it. Don't dress too nicely, there's a lot of setup work involved."

Dawn nodded, already regretting her decision but committed now, trapped by her own words and her family's expectations.

Outside, snow began to fall, the first snow of the season, covering Holly Falls in postcard perfection.

Dawn watched it through the kitchen window and wondered if she was looking at three weeks of Christmas magic or three weeks of slowly suffocating under the weight of everyone's good intentions.

More than likely, it will be both.

Chapter 2:
The Unmade Wish

Dawn needed air. Twenty-four hours of family togetherness had reached her natural saturation point somewhere between her mother's second breakfast offering and Amy's color-coded timeline for festival preparation. The Donovan house smelled like nutmeg and felt like maternal expectations, and Dawn was suffocating on both. She could not handle the stress a moment longer.

"I'm going for a walk," she announced, grabbing her camera bag and jacket.

"It's cold out there," Patricia called from the kitchen, where she was doing something that involved a lot of clanging and what sounded like competitive baking. "You need a proper coat. And gloves. And probably a hat."

"I have a jacket."

"That jacket wouldn't keep a hamster warm in July."

Amy emerged from the living room, clipboard in hand, wearing the expression of someone who had "Lists" and wasn't afraid to use them. "Where are you walking to?"

"Just into town. Getting my bearings. Maybe I'll grab a coffee."

"The Busy Bean has excellent coffee," Patricia added helpfully. "And they know you there. Mrs. Henderson always asks about you."

Because of course they did. In Holly Falls, being known was inescapable. Dawn had spent ten years cultivating anonymity in a dozen different cities, perfecting the art of being a stranger. Coming home meant being instantly recognizable again, being the Donovan girl who left and kept leaving.

"I'll be back in an hour," Dawn said, already heading for the door before anyone could suggest she take a thermos, dress more appropriately, or think about any of the seventeen safety concerns that small-town mothers are known for.

The November air hit her like a wake-up call, sharp and clean, carrying the promise of snow. Holly Falls stretched out before her in familiar patterns: tree-lined streets, well-maintained sidewalks, houses that looked like they'd been designed by someone who believed deeply in the concept of curb appeal.

And Christmas decorations. Everywhere. Like the town decorator had a seizure with the decoration boxes.

It was still five days before Thanksgiving, but Holly Falls had apparently decided that seasonal restraint was for amateurs. Every lamppost sported a garland collar. Every storefront window vied for the title of Most Aggressively Festive. The town square ahead sparkled as if someone had sneezed tinsel across the entire landscape.

Dawn pulled out her phone, partly to record the holiday chaos and partly to avoid making eye contact with the neighbors who would want to stop and chat. Mrs. Patterson was visible through her front window, clearly positioning herself to get a glimpse of Dawn. Father Newman was raking leaves with the kind of precision that suggested he had been waiting for a reason to pause and catch up.

Dawn typed a text to Maya, who was probably still asleep at the Holly Falls Inn: *Town has been overrun with Christmas cheer. Send help. Or at least coffee.*

Maya's response was swift: *Embrace the holiday chaos. Take pictures. I want proof of this small-town holiday madness.*

Dawn was composing a response about the inflatable snowman epidemic when she backed into someone.

Hard.

The impact knocked her phone from her hand and sent her stumbling backward into something solid and warm and definitely human. Strong hands caught her shoulders, steadying her before she could complete her graceless tumble.

"Whoa there. You okay?"

The voice was familiar. Too familiar. Dawn's stomach did a complicated flip before she even turned around.

Jack Harrison stood behind her, hands still on her shoulders, wearing a smile that was warm and uncomplicated and exactly the same as it had been two years ago. He'd filled out some in the two years since she'd seen him, broader shoulders, laugh lines around his eyes, but he was unmistakably Jack. Unmistakably, the man who'd watched her leave town with an expression she'd tried very hard not to remember.

"Dawn." His smile widened, and there wasn't a trace of bitterness in it, just genuine pleasure. "I heard you were back in town."

Jack. Hi." Dawn took a step back, creating some space between them that felt both necessary and silly. "Sorry about that. I was texting, which is exactly the kind of thing my mother would tell me not to do."

"No harm done. Though you might want to…" He pointed down.

Dawn looked down. Her phone was on the sidewalk next to small snow boots, a tiny backpack decorated with cartoon unicorns, and a folder that seemed to hold school projects.

A little girl stood by the sidewalk debris, looking up at Dawn with the kind of honest curiosity that only seven-year-olds have. She was clearly Jack's daughter, with the same dark eyes and the same direct gaze, but smaller than Dawn remembered. More real. The last time Dawn had seen Lily Harrison, she was barely more than a toddler. Now she's a young girl with opinions, peacoats, and apparently a part in the school Christmas play.

"Lily," Jack said gently, "this is Dawn. She was a friend of Daddy's a couple of years ago."

"I remember. Hi," Lily said solemnly. "Did you drop your phone because you were walking backward?"

"I did. That was poor planning on my part."

"Mama used to do that. Before." Lily's matter-of-fact tone made Jack's expression tighten slightly. "She said walking and texting was like trying to pat your head and rub your belly at the same time, but harder."

Dawn's chest tightened. Jack's wife, Claudia, who had died three years ago from a fast-spreading cancer—one that medicine and miracles couldn't stop—was a reminder of the past. Dawn had heard about her from Amy, who had gotten the news from their mother, who collected information about Holly Falls residents the way some people gather stamps.

"Your mama sounds like she was smart," Dawn said carefully.

"She was. She also made really good pancakes." Lily picked up Dawn's phone and handed it to her with the grave responsibility of someone returning a valued possession. "Are you visiting for Thanksgiving?"

"For Christmas. Maybe longer."

"How come you never come visit us?"

The question hit Dawn like a gentle but firm blow. Jack's face became carefully neutral, resembling a parent trying not to influence their child's social questioning while ready to step in if needed.

Dawn crouched down to Lily's eye level, buying herself time to figure out how to explain a decade of deliberate distance to a seven-year-old. "I travel a lot for work. I take pictures in different places."

"Like vacation pictures?"

"Sort of. Pictures for magazines and websites. So other people can see pretty places they might want to visit."

"That sounds fun." Lily considered this. "But don't you get lonely? Daddy says traveling is fun, but home is where people miss you."

Dawn's throat tightened. Out of the mouths of babes and seven-year-olds with an alarming grasp of emotional truth. "Sometimes. But I like seeing new places."

"We're late for rehearsal," Jack said gently, reading the conversation's trajectory and stepping in before his daughter could ask any more devastating questions. "Lily's playing an angel in the Christmas pageant."

"An important angel," Lily corrected. "I get to hold the star."

"Very important," Dawn agreed, standing back up. Her knees felt unsteady, though whether from crouching or from the weight of Lily's innocent observations, she couldn't tell.

"Maybe I'll see you around," Jack said. "The festival, or... your mom mentioned you might be helping with setup."

"Maybe. Yeah."

Jack scooped up Lily's backpack and script, then lifted her onto his shoulders in one smooth motion that spoke of practice and routine. "Say bye to Dawn, Lil."

"Bye, Dawn. Maybe next time you can come over and see my room. I have a fish."

Dawn watched them walk away, Jack's steady stride, Lily's small hand waving over his head until they disappeared around the corner toward the elementary school. The ordinary sight of a father and daughter going about their Thursday morning routine. The accumulation of small rituals that made a life.

This is what she'd walked away from. Not Jack specifically, she'd liked him, genuinely cared about him, but she hadn't loved him the way he'd deserved. She'd known that even with the short amount of time they spent together two years ago. But this: the small hand, the peacoat, the fish in a bedroom she'd never see. The way Lily spoke about her mother in present tense sometimes and past tense other times, like grief was something you navigated rather than something you got over.

Dawn found a bench in the town square and sat down abruptly. Her phone buzzed with texts—Maya asking for updates, Amy wondering where she was—but she ignored them. Instead, she fixated on the massive Christmas tree that towered in the center of the square, already outlined with white lights even though it wouldn't be officially lit until after Thanksgiving.

Her phone rang. Amy.

"Where are you?" Amy's voice carried the tone of someone who'd already checked three logical locations and was moving on to mild panic.

"Town square. On a bench. Having an existential crisis."

"What kind of existential crisis? The 'I shouldn't have come home' kind, or the 'I should never leave home' kind?"

"The 'I just ran into Jack, and Lily asked me why I never visit' kind."

Silence. Then: "Ouch."

"She has a fish, Amy. She wanted to show me her room and tell me about her fish."

"And that's bad because...?"

"It's not bad. It's—" Dawn pressed her free hand to her forehead. "It's real. It's the kind of real I don't do."

"Maybe it's time you learned."

"Says the woman who color-codes her spice rack."

"My spice rack organization has nothing to do with your commitment phobia."

Dawn's laugh came out sharper than she'd intended. "Everything is about my commitment phobia, according to this family. I can't organize spices without it being a statement about my relationship patterns."

"That's because your relationship patterns involve fleeing whenever someone suggests you might want to stick around."

"I don't flee. I relocate strategically."

"You fled Austin because someone wanted to share a spice drawer."

"That's different. That was—" Dawn paused. "Okay, that was fleeing."

"Come home," Amy said, her voice gentling. "Mom found the wish ornaments."

Dawn's stomach dropped. "No. Absolutely not. I'm not doing the wish thing."

"It's tradition."

"Tradition is peer pressure from dead people."

"Nana's ornament, Dawn. The one with the little door. You know how much this means to Mom."

Dawn knew. The wish ornament had belonged to their grandmother, a delicate glass sphere with a tiny hinged door where you could tuck a folded paper with your secret wish. Every year, Patricia insisted on the ritual: write your wish, fold it small, put it in the ornament, hang it on the tree. The wishes weren't read until New Year's Day, when the family would gather around the tree and share what they'd hoped for.

It was sweet. It was meaningful. It was exactly the kind of binding, traditional, commitment-laden family ritual that made Dawn want to book the next flight to anywhere else.

"I don't have anything to wish for," Dawn lied.

"Everyone has something to wish for."

"Fine. I wish for this conversation to end."

"Dawn—"

"I'm coming. Give me ten minutes."

Dawn hung up and sat for another moment on the bench, watching Holly Falls go about its Thursday morning business. Mrs. Newman was walking her ancient beagle past the gazebo. A teenager on a bike delivered papers to the shops around the square. Two women chatted near the fountain, their voices carrying in the crisp air.

Ordinary life. The kind of life that accumulated slowly, built from small traditions and daily routines, and fish in bedrooms and daughters who asked direct questions about why people didn't visit.

She took out her phone and texted Maya: *I changed my mind. Heading home. See you later.*

Dawn walked home slowly, taking the long way past the elementary school where she could hear children's voices from the playground, past the fire station where Jack worked, past the coffee shop where Mrs. Henderson would definitely want to chat about how good it was to have her back in town.

At home, she saw her family arranged around the kitchen table like they were staging a Norman Rockwell scene. Doug sat at one end, struggling with a string of lights that had apparently been tangled for years. Patricia stood at the counter, rolling out pie crust with the focused intensity of someone preparing for a battle. Amy sat at the table with her clipboard, naturally, but she had also laid Nana's ornament on a small plate as if it was a sacred artifact.

Which, Dawn supposed, it was.

The ornament was exactly as she remembered: glass blown thin as a soap bubble, painted with tiny holly leaves and berries, with a small brass door that opened on whisper-quiet hinges. Inside, rolled paper wishes from Christmases past had left faint impressions on the glass walls.

"There you are," Patricia said without looking up from her pie crust. "I was starting to worry you'd gotten lost. Or decided to run off to another continent."

"Just town. I ran into Jack."

Amy looked up from her clipboard. "How is he?"

"Good. Lily's in the Christmas pageant. She's playing an angel."

"That's sweet." Patricia's voice carried the careful neutrality of someone who had opinions about Dawn's romantic history but was trying not to share them. "Jack's a good father."

"He is." Dawn sat down across from Amy, eyeing the ornament as if it might bite her. "So. The wishes."

"Family tradition," Doug said, looking up from his light-tangling project. "Your grandmother started it when your mom and I were first married. Been doing it ever since."

"It's not a blood oath," Amy added, reading Dawn's expression. "It's just... intention setting. Putting something you want out into the universe."

"It feels like a blood oath."

"That's the commitment issues talking."

Dawn picked up the ornament, turning it carefully in her hands. The glass was warm from the kitchen, smooth except for the tiny raised holly pattern. Through the little door, she could see the shadows of old wishes, paper ghosts of Christmases past.

"What did you wish for last year?" she asked Amy.

Amy's cheeks flushed slightly. "Someone who'd see the real me. Not the organized, in-control version. The messy, uncertain, sometimes-anxious version." She paused. "And then Will happened."

"Will sees your messy version?"

"Will prefers my messy version. Says the clipboard is adorable but the woman behind it is what he fell for."

Dawn stared at her sister. Amy, who color-coded everything, who made lists for her lists, who approached life like a project that could be managed into submission, had wished for someone who'd love her chaos. And gotten him.

"Maybe the wish isn't magic," Amy continued. "Maybe it's permission. To want something. To admit what you actually need instead of what you think you should want."

Patricia rolled her pie crust with particular vigor. "I just want both my daughters to be happy. That's been my wish for thirty years running."

"What about you, Dad?" Dawn asked.

Doug held up his string of lights, which had somehow become more tangled during their conversation. "I wish for Christmas lights that don't have personal vendettas against me. And for my daughters to figure out that happiness isn't something you find, it's something you build."

Amy slid a piece of paper across the table to Dawn. "Your turn."

34

Dawn picked up the pen Amy offered, then stared at the blank paper. What did she want? Really want, underneath all the deflection and humor and strategic exits?

A place to land, she wrote quickly, before she could overthink it. Someone who won't make me stay, but maybe wants to go with me.

The words seemed contradictory on paper. Impossible. A place to land implied stopping, settling, and choosing somewhere to be. Someone who won't make me stay suggested freedom, escape routes, and the ability to leave when things got complicated. And someone to go with me? Where did that come from?

But it felt true. Truer than anything she'd written in years.

Dawn folded the paper small, opened the little brass door, and tucked her wish inside. The door closed with a tiny click that sounded, in the warm kitchen, like a promise.

"Done," she said.

"That's it?" Amy asked. "No crisis? No speech about how wishes are just psychological manipulation disguised as family bonding?"

"I'm saving that for later. When the wish doesn't come true, I can say I told you so."

Patricia laughed, her first genuinely relaxed sound since Dawn had arrived. "Oh, sweetheart. You have no idea how the universe works, do you?"

That night, Dawn lay in her childhood bedroom, staring at the glow-in-the-dark stars still stuck to the ceiling from when she was twelve. Downstairs, Nana's ornament hung on the Christmas tree, holding her impossible wish. A place to land. Someone who won't make me stay.

She'd made a wish like a child. Felt ridiculous and hopeful and terrified in equal measure.

Her phone buzzed. A text from Maya: *How's the family therapy disguised as holiday traditions?*

Dawn typed back: *Made a wish. Might be legally binding. Will keep you posted.*

Maya: *What did you wish for?*

Dawn stared at the phone, then at the stars on her ceiling. *Something impossible.*

Maya: *Those are the only wishes worth making.*

Dawn turned over, pulling her childhood quilt up to her chin. Somewhere downstairs, her wish sat in its glass sphere, waiting for Christmas magic or cosmic intervention or whatever force made small-town Christmas miracles possible.

She'd wished for contradiction: stability and freedom, landing and leaving, someone who'd let her stay without making her feel trapped, or go with her.

It was impossible.

It was exactly what she wanted.

Outside her window, Holly Falls slept under the promise of snow, and Dawn closed her eyes and tried not to hope too hard.

Chapter 3:
The Crash on Main Street

Dawn had a mission. She wasn't wandering around Holly Falls out of restlessness, not because her mother's house felt too warm and full of expectations, or because Amy's clipboard efficiency made her feel like a particularly chaotic houseguest. She was working. Documenting. Being productive.

The travel piece she had pitched to *Midwest Living* six months ago and never started suddenly became urgent. Holly Falls in winter would make excellent content, small-town charm, Christmas traditions, the kind of place city dwellers fantasize about during their commutes. She could frame it as *"The Perfect Holiday Getaway," "Christmas Done Right,"* or some other magazine-friendly angle that would justify the time she was spending here.

That she was probably going to spend here whether she worked or not was beside the point.

The Busy Bean buzzed with the unique energy of a small-town coffee shop that doubled as an unofficial community hub. Dawn pushed through the door, inhaling the aroma of coffee and cinnamon, and listening to the faint local gossip. Mrs. Henderson, behind the counter, looked up from the espresso machine and smiled.

"Dawn Donovan! Twice in one week. We're getting spoiled."

"Just picking up supplies," Dawn said, approaching the counter where her art supply order waited, sketch pads, charcoal, and the good colored pencils she had ordered online and shipped here because planning ahead was apparently something she could do when it involved avoiding emotional conversations.

"Your mother mentioned you might be working on an article about the town. That's wonderful. We could use the publicity." Mrs. Henderson handed Dawn's order along with two gingerbread lattes. "One for Amy?"

"Bribery coffee. She's been very patient with my complete inability to commit to anything other than a grocery list."

"Sisters." Mrs. Henderson's tone suggested a deep understanding of sibling dynamics. "Mine once made me alphabetize her books because I accidentally borrowed one without asking."

Dawn balanced her portfolio case, the bag of art supplies, and both lattes while trying to fish her phone from her pocket. Amy had texted three times in the last hour, which either meant clipboard emergency or that their mother had discovered Dawn's lack of a return flight and was spiraling into protective overdrive.

Amy: *Where are you?*

Amy: *Mom's making her worried face. ETA?*

Amy: *Also we need to discuss your complete lack of winter coats. Your jacket is decorative at best.*

Dawn typed back one-handed: *Have coffee. Coming home. The jacket is vintage and has character.*

She backed toward the café door, still texting, because multitasking was a skill she'd perfected during her nomadic years. The key was maintaining forward momentum while handling three different tasks, which required—

She slammed into something solid.

The impact was spectacular. One gingerbread latte launched itself into the air like it had been catapulted. Her portfolio case hit the sidewalk and slid across the snow-slicked pavement. Art supplies were scattered like colorful refugees fleeing a disaster zone.

Dawn spun around, already apologizing, and found herself face-to-chest with someone who was also no longer holding what he'd been holding. Boxes—three of them—now decorated the sidewalk. One had split open, spilling silver tinsel and glass ornaments across the snow, where they mixed with her colored pencils in a chaotic holiday crime scene.

"Oh God. Oh no. I'm so sorry, I wasn't—I was texting, which I know makes me the worst person in town—"

She looked up.

The man staring back at her had paint on his hands. Old paint, the kind that survived multiple scrubbings but never quite came out of the creases around fingernails and knuckles. Dawn knew that stain intimately. She had that stain.

But everything else about him was confusing. His coat was expensive, likely cashmere, probably the kind that costs more than most people's rent, but it was rumpled, as if he'd slept in it. Or maybe hadn't slept at all. His dark hair was doing something that looked either intentionally tousled or the result of him running his hands through it repeatedly. He looked like someone who had been carefully put together this morning but had since gone through something that involved a lot of stress, and possibly a minor disaster.

He also had whipped cream on his left eyebrow.

"You have—" Dawn gestured at her own eyebrow.

He touched his face, found the cream, and examined it on his fingers with a look of genuine bewilderment. Then he laughed, and it was a hearty laugh, surprised and genuine, the kind that made his eyes crinkle.

"Well," he said. "That's a new one."

His voice had a slight rasp to it, like he'd been talking for hours or hadn't had enough coffee yet. There was something familiar about it, though Dawn was sure she'd never seen him before. She would have remembered the paint stains, if nothing else.

"Your latte," she said unnecessarily, gesturing at the whipped cream evidence.

"My fault for being in the path of a guided missile."

"I was not… okay, I was absolutely a guided missile. But an apologetic one." Dawn dropped to her knees on the cold sidewalk, collecting scattered pencils. "I'll pay for the ornaments. And dry cleaning. And therapy if you need it after being assaulted by coffee."

He knelt beside her, gathering tinsel that sparkled like festive confetti. "The ornaments were already fragile. Consider it natural selection."

Dawn looked up from rescuing a purple pencil from a small snowdrift. He was close enough that she could see his eyes, brown, with little flecks of gold that caught the light. Also close enough to notice that his expensive coat smelled like sawdust and something that might have been paint thinner.

"You're not from around here," she said.

"What gave it away? The fact that I don't know how to avoid texting pedestrians, or the general aura of confusion?"

"The coat. It's too nice for Holly Falls in December. We're more of a flannel and practical footwear town." She held up a shattered glass ornament. "This one's giving very abstract art now."

"I could say it was intentional. Very... deconstructionist."

Dawn grinned despite herself. "You know art terms. That's dangerous."

"I know a lot of mostly useless things. It's a condition." Thomas, though she didn't know his name yet, noticed her portfolio case, which had flopped open to reveal sketches and the sticker she'd stuck to the inside cover: *I put the 'pro' in 'procrastinate.'*

"A fellow professional," he said, pointing to the sticker.

"World class. I've been planning this article for six months. Today I finally bought supplies."

"What's the article about?"

"Small-town Christmas magic. Or Christmas madness. I haven't decided which angle yet."

They were both still on their knees, collecting the aftermath of their collision. Dawn noticed that Thomas had good hands, long fingers, careful movements, the kind of hands that looked like they knew how to fix things. But the paint stains didn't match the expensive coat, and there was something too careful about the way he handled the broken ornaments, like he wasn't used to cleaning up messes.

"Are you visiting for the holidays?" Dawn asked.

"Something like that. I'm helping with the Christmas festival. Volunteering."

"You picked the right town. Holly Falls takes Christmas very seriously. It's like living inside a snow globe from December first through New Year's."

"So I'm discovering." He held up a piece of tinsel that had somehow gotten wound around one of her pencils. "Is this performance art?"

"If I say yes, will you help me think of a title?"

"*'Collision Course: A Study in Gravity and Poor Timing.'*"

Dawn laughed, which was a mistake because it made her lose track of what she was supposed to be collecting. "That's either very pretentious or very honest."

"Both. The best art usually is."

Before Dawn could respond to that, and she definitely wanted to respond because anyone who could make philosophical observations about art while kneeling in slush was worth further conversation, the café door burst open.

"What happened out here?" Mrs. Henderson appeared, dish towel in hand, surveying the scene like a general assessing a battlefield. "It sounds like someone dropped Santa's workshop."

"Minor collision," Dawn said, standing up and brushing snow off her knees. "My fault entirely."

"Our fault," Thomas corrected, also standing. "I was in the way."

Mrs. Henderson looked between them, then at the scattered remains of their respective burdens, and her expression shifted into something that might have been calculation. "Well. Since you're both here, and since my decorator just called in sick with the flu, you can help me with the window display contest."

"Oh, we don't need to—" Dawn started.

"Nonsense. You made the mess, you can help clean up a different mess. The contest judging is in two hours, and I'm competing against Marta's place next door. She's been smug about her *'Winter Wonderland'* theme all week." Mrs. Henderson's competitive spirit was clearly engaged. "I need all hands."

Dawn looked at Thomas. Thomas looked at Dawn. They both looked at Mrs. Henderson, who had the expression of someone who would not be taking no for an answer.

"What does helping involve, exactly?" Thomas asked cautiously.

"Decorating. How hard can it be?"

Famous last words, Dawn thought, but she found herself nodding. "One hour. Then I really do need to get home before my family sends out a search party."

"Perfect." Mrs. Henderson beamed and disappeared back inside, returning with boxes of decorations that seemed to reproduce themselves when no one was looking. "I'm thinking *'Cozy Christmas Café.'* Warm, inviting, makes people want to drink things."

"Good marketing strategy," Dawn said.

"I like her already," Thomas murmured.

For the next hour, Dawn learned several things about her collision partner. First, he had too many impractical ideas and a kind of enthusiasm that suggested he'd never actually had to carry any of them out. Second, he was methodical about the strangest things; he arranged tinsel by length and color before hanging it, and he checked the symmetry of every garland placement, but he seemed completely baffled by basic tools.

He held the staple gun as if it might bite him. Turned it over, tested the trigger in the air, frowned as if it were whispering secrets he couldn't understand. When she handed him a strand of lights, he squinted at the plug as if it insulted him, then asked where the batteries were. There were no batteries.

She let him climb the stepladder just once. Only once. He leaned too far to the left, chasing the perfect angle for a crooked snowflake decal, and nearly toppled into a display of ceramic mugs shaped like reindeer butts. After that, she told him to stay on the ground and handed him suction cups as if she were arming a toddler for battle.

Still, he had a certain stubborn charm. When the cold nipped at their fingers and the wind rattled the window glass, he kept humming some off-key version of "Deck the Halls" and smiling as if he belonged in a snow globe. When the suction cups refused to hold the candy cane garland, he stuck them anyway, rearranging until the weight balanced just right. Dawn watched him work, haphazard but oddly precise, and realized he wasn't trying to decorate a window. He was trying to tell a story. One about magic and mischief, the kind that makes people pause and smile despite the bitter cold.

By the time they stepped back to admire the scene, Santa's sleigh was suspended mid-flight, tinsel comets trailing behind like silver fire, her fingertips ached and her patience had thinned to floss. But the window glowed. It pulsed with whimsy and some inexplicable sense of hope. And for the first time all week, she didn't mind the snow.

"Have you ever used a staple gun before?" Dawn asked, watching him stare at the device as if it might bite him.

"I've seen them being used before," he said carefully.

"That's not the same thing."

"No, it's really not."

She showed him how to load it, how to hold it, and how to aim for the corner of the garland instead of his thumb. He was a quick learner, but there was something strangely formal about the way he approached it, as if he were learning a skill he never thought he'd need.

"What do you do for work?" Dawn asked, draping lights around the window frame while Thomas wrestled with a particularly stubborn strand of garland.

"Management consulting," he said, which was technically accurate but felt like an evasion. "Problem-solving. Strategy. What about you?"

"Photography, mostly. Travel writing, when I can sell it. Occasional mural work." Dawn glanced at his hands again. "What kind of consulting involves paint?"

"The hands-on kind?"

She was about to ask for details when Thomas's phone buzzed. He looked at it, and something changed in his expression, a tension she hadn't seen before.

"I should probably—" he started.

"Go ahead. I can finish up here."

Thomas looked at his phone again, then at Dawn, then seemed to make a decision. "Actually, it can wait. How does this look?"

He'd managed to create a garland swag that was perfectly symmetrical and completely impractical. Beautiful, but the kind of beautiful that wouldn't survive the first strong wind.

"Very elegant. Completely non-functional, but elegant."

"Story of my life," Thomas said, and there was something in his tone that made Dawn look at him more closely.

Before she could ask what he meant, Mrs. Henderson stepped out of the café to check their work. "Oh, this is lovely! Much better than Marta's disco ball nightmare next door." She smiled at them. "You two make a good team."

Dawn felt her cheeks flush. "We're not—this was just—"

"You should enter the gingerbread house contest next weekend. It's couples only."

"We just met," Dawn said quickly. "Literally an hour ago. Via collision."

Some of the best relationships begin with a good crash," Mrs. Henderson said wisely. "My Harold and I met when I rear-ended his truck at a stop sign. Forty-three years next month."

Thomas checked his watch, and it was a nice watch, Dawn noticed, definitely nicer than his story about consulting suggested. "I should probably let you get home," he said to Dawn. "Your family's probably worried."

"Probably," Dawn agreed, though she found herself reluctant to end the conversation. "Are you sticking around town for a while?"

"A few weeks. Through the holidays, at least." Thomas helped her gather her art supplies, which had somehow multiplied during their decoration adventure. "I'm sure I'll see you around. Holly Falls seems like the kind of place where you run into the same people repeatedly."

"Usually when you're trying to avoid them," Dawn said. "But sometimes it works out."

They stood there for a moment, surrounded by the debris of their crash and the aftermath of their impromptu decorating project. Dawn realized she didn't know his name, and now it seemed too late to ask without appearing completely clueless.

"Well," she said finally. "Thanks for helping with my crash landing. And for not calling the police when I assaulted you with coffee."

"Thanks for making my first week in Holly Falls memorable," Thomas said as he handed her the portfolio case. "Good luck with your article."

"Good luck with your... consulting."

Dawn walked away, her portfolio damp, her latte cold, and glitter somehow stuck in her hair despite her best efforts to avoid it. She caught herself smiling, which was ridiculous. She had literally crashed into a stranger and spent an hour hanging tinsel, and somehow it had been the most fun she's had since arriving in Holly Falls.

She was halfway home when she realized she'd never gotten his name.

She was almost to her parents' house when she realized she didn't actually mind.

Her phone buzzed with a text from Amy: *Where's my bribery coffee?*

Dawn looked down at the single surviving latte, which had gone cold and was probably undrinkable. *Casualties of war. I'll explain when I get home.*

Amy: *This better be a good story.*

Dawn thought about paint-stained hands and expensive coats and the way he'd laughed when he found whipped cream on his eyebrow. About how he'd arranged tinsel by color and asked thoughtful questions about her work and somehow made decorating a coffee shop window feel like the most important thing they could be doing.

It was definitely going to be a good story.

She just wasn't sure how it was going to end.

Chapter 4:
The Volunteer Trap

Dawn was having a perfectly peaceful afternoon before Amy ruined it. She'd finally found her rhythm, spread out across her parents' dining room table with sketch pads and colored pencils, working on preliminary drawings for what might become either a travel article or a mural proposal for the mayor. The late afternoon light was perfect, streaming through the windows and illuminating her workspace like a blessing. For the first time since arriving in Holly Falls, she felt productive rather than restless.

Then Amy appeared in the doorway holding two coats.

"Get up. We're going."

Dawn didn't look up from her sketch of the town square gazebo. "I'm working."

"You're procrastinating with extra steps to make it last longer. There's a difference." Amy tossed Dawn's jacket at her head with the precision of someone who'd perfected sibling warfare decades ago. "Town meeting. Festival planning. Remember? I need backup. "

"Backup for what? You have a clipboard. You have multiple clipboards. You're the most prepared person in any room you've ever entered." Dawn continued sketching and adding shading to the gazebo's Victorian details. "You don't need backup. You need subordinates."

"Moral support," Amy said firmly, already heading for the door with the confidence of someone who expected to be followed. "Also, since you told me you would help, I may have told Mayor Posey you'd be there."

Dawn's pencil stopped moving. "Amy."

"She's very excited to meet you. Apparently, Mom's been talking about your *artistic vision.*" Amy made air quotes that were somehow both encouraging and threatening. "You have fifteen minutes to look like someone with artistic vision. Let's go."

Dawn stared at her sister. "What exactly did Mom tell her about my artistic vision?"

"That you're talented, creative, temporarily available, and in need of community engagement to prevent you from fleeing the state before Christmas dinner."

"She didn't say that last part."

"She didn't have to. I'm translating from Patricia Donovan." Amy checked her watch. "Fourteen minutes now."

Dawn looked at her sketch pad, then at Amy's expectant face, and finally at the coat that had been used as a weapon against her productivity. The smart move would be to refuse. To stay here with her art supplies and her perfectly manageable afternoon, avoiding whatever trap Amy was setting.

But Amy had used the phrase "temporarily available," which suggested their mother was actively marketing Dawn's presence in Holly Falls to anyone who would listen. Which meant hiding at home was only delaying the inevitable.

"One hour," Dawn said, standing up and reaching for her jacket. "I'll give you one hour, and then I'm coming back here to finish my work."

"Deal."

They walked to the town hall along streets glittering with early Christmas decorations. Not a lamppost was left undecorated. Every storefront window vied for the most festive display. It was beautiful, overwhelming, and just the kind of small-town perfection that made Dawn feel like she was inside a snow globe.

"So what exactly happens at a festival planning meeting?" Dawn asked.

"Committees assign tasks. Budgets are debated. Mrs. Patterson tries to ban the Henderson twins from the cookie booth again." Amy consulted her clipboard while walking, which was a skill that never failed to impress Dawn. "Also, they're searching for new gala co-chairs."

Dawn stopped walking. "Amy."

"What?"

"You're not thinking of volunteering me for something, are you?"

Amy's expression was perfectly, suspiciously neutral. "I would never volunteer you for anything without your consent."

"That's not a no."

"That's not a yes, either."

Dawn studied her sister's face. Amy had the same expression she'd worn at age eight when she'd convinced Dawn to trade Halloween candy, innocent, helpful, and definitely planning something. "I'm not co-chairing anything. I don't co-chair. I barely chair myself most days."

"Noted," Amy said, which wasn't the firm agreement Dawn was hoping for.

The community center was alive with the unique energy of a small town coming together. Folding chairs were organized in tidy rows, a refreshment table was stocked with plenty of cookie options, and at least three people sported over-the-top Christmas sweaters, hopefully one of a kind. Dawn tried to find a spot in the back row, blending in with the crowd.

Amy dragged her to the second row.

"Backup," Amy said firmly when Dawn protested. "You can't provide backup from the cheap seats."

Mayor Karen Posey commanded the front of the room with the energy of someone who had consumed her body weight in holiday spirit. She was reviewing festival logistics with military precision, parade routes, vendor permits, safety protocols, and what seemed to be an alarming amount of bureaucracy for a town of eight thousand people.

Dawn was scanning the room for alternate exit routes when the community center door opened.

Thomas walked in.

He looked around the room, clearly uncertain about the seating politics of small-town meetings, and his eyes found Dawn. His face lit up with a private, warm smile, as if they shared a secret. Which, technically, they did; yesterday's collision and coffee shop rescue mission felt like something that had happened only to them.

Dawn looked away too quickly, pretending to study her agenda with intense concentration.

"Who's that?" Amy asked immediately.

"No one."

"You're blushing."

"I'm warm. It's stuffy in here."

Amy glanced around the spacious room, which had excellent ventilation. "It's sixty-two degrees. I glanced at the thermostat when we walked in."

Before Dawn could craft a response that didn't involve admitting she'd spent forty-five minutes yesterday hanging tinsel with a stranger, Mayor Posey called for attention.

"Before we move to committee reports, I'd like to introduce our volunteer coordinator for this year's festival." The mayor gestured toward Thomas, who stood up with the kind of easy confidence that suggested he was comfortable being the center of attention. "Thomas Miller has generously offered his time and expertise to help us pull together what I'm sure will be our best Christmas celebration yet."

Thomas gave a small wave to the room. "Thank you for welcoming me to Holly Falls. I've been impressed by the community's dedication to making this season special. There's something rare about places like this, where people know one another, where traditions matter, and where everyone contributes to something bigger than themselves."

There was something rehearsed about the speech. Not insincere, exactly, but deliberate. Like he'd given similar talks in other settings, to other groups. Dawn found herself studying his face, searching for tells.

"Thomas comes to us with extensive event management experience," Mayor Posey continued, "and he's staying in Holly Falls through the holidays. We're lucky to have him."

Polite applause. Thomas sat back down, briefly catching Dawn's eye again. This time, she didn't look away immediately, and she felt her cheeks warm under his gaze.

"Now," Mayor Posey said, consulting her clipboard with the focused intensity of a general reviewing battle plans, "we have some exciting news about the Snowball Gala."

Dawn's stomach began to sink before she understood why.

"Unfortunately, our original co-chairs have had to step aside due to family circumstances. Which means we need two new leaders for what's traditionally our signature event."

The room was paying attention now. Dawn could feel the weight of collective expectation, the way communities looked for volunteers. She slumped further in her chair, trying to become invisible through her posture.

"The gala needs people with creativity, organizational skills, and availability." Mayor Posey's eyes swept the room and landed on Dawn like a heat-seeking missile. "Dawn Donovan."

Dawn's blood turned to ice. "I—yes?"

"Your mother tells me you're an artist."

"I mean, technically, but—"

"And you're here through Christmas, correct?"

Dawn thought about her unbooked return flight. About the fact that she'd told Amy she might stay through New Year's. About the way her family kept assuming she'd be here for major events, like she was someone who stayed in one place. "I... yes, but I'm not sure I'm the right person for—"

"Wonderful." Mayor Posey jotted something down on her clipboard with the certainty of someone closing a deal. "And Thomas, you've already shown great initiative with the festival planning. How would you feel about co-chairing the gala with Dawn?"

Every head in the room turned to look at Thomas, then at Dawn, then back to Thomas as if they were watching a slow-motion tennis match. Dawn could hear her own heartbeat.

Thomas looked straight at her, his face unreadable. "If Dawn's comfortable with that arrangement, I'd be honored."

The silence stretched like taffy. Dawn was keenly aware that forty-seven people were waiting for her answer. That Amy was sitting beside her with suspiciously perfect posture. That Thomas was still looking at her with that steady, patient gaze.

She had about three seconds to escape. She could say she had a prior commitment, a family emergency, or a sudden case of laryngitis. She looked at Amy for help.

Amy's face was perfectly, deliberately, neutral.

"I..." Dawn's mouth felt full of cotton. "I'm only here temporarily. I don't want to commit to something I can't follow through on."

"The gala is Christmas Eve," Mayor Posey said smoothly. "You'll be here Christmas Eve, won't you?"

It wasn't really a question. It was the kind of gentle assumption small towns made about their own, that family and community obligations would naturally keep you tethered to the important moments.

Dawn thought about Christmas Eve. About the family dinner, midnight mass, and how her mother's face lit up when both daughters were home for the holidays. She reflected on the fact that she'd never actually missed a Christmas Eve in Holly Falls, no matter how far she'd run or how long she'd stayed away.

"...Yes."

"Then it's settled." Mayor Posey beamed with the satisfaction of someone who'd successfully matched compatible volunteers. "Dawn and Thomas, our Snowball Gala co-chairs. Let's give them a hand."

Applause. Actual, enthusiastic applause. Dawn was definitely going to kill Amy.

After the meeting broke into smaller committee groups, Dawn found herself standing with Thomas near the refreshment table, both of them holding folders of gala information they hadn't requested.

"So," Thomas said, flipping through a packet that appeared to contain seventeen different spreadsheets, "looks like we're stuck together."

"Looks like." Dawn examined her own folder with the expression of someone who had accidentally volunteered to climb Everest. Venue logistics. Budget breakdowns. Vendor contracts. Timeline charts. This was a serious commitment. This was weeks of planning, coordination, and follow-through. What had she done?

"For what it's worth," Thomas said, "I didn't plan this."

She looked up. His expression was genuine, maybe slightly amused. "I didn't think you did."

"Though I'm not sorry about it," he said simply, as if he were stating an obvious fact. Like being partnered with her was something he'd actively choose rather than something he'd been forced into.

Dawn wasn't sure how to handle that much direct honesty, so she did what she always did when conversations became too serious: deflected with self-deprecation.

"Fair warning, I'm terrible at this. Organizing. Planning. Following through on commitments." She gestured vaguely at the folder. "I'm more of a 'show up with impossible ideas and then disappear before implementation' type of person."

"Noted." Thomas didn't seem concerned. "I'm decent at implementation. We might balance each other out."

"Or we'll be a complete disaster."

"Also possible." He was smiling now, and it was the kind of smile that made the corners of his eyes crinkle. "But at least it'll be interesting."

They ended up walking in the same direction after the meeting, with Dawn heading home and Thomas heading toward the town center where she assumed he was staying. Holly Falls was small enough that most paths converged, which was either convenient or the universe's way of encouraging maximum social entanglement.

56

They walked slowly, neither of them rushing to get where they were going.

"Can I ask you something?" Dawn said as they passed the coffee shop where they'd first crashed into each other.

"Sure."

"Why are you really here? In Holly Falls, I mean."

Thomas paused for a moment, thoughtfully considering his response like someone who's been asked this question before. "My family has a history with this town," he said finally. "Charitable work, mostly. I wanted to see it in person instead of just as a name on a check."

"So you're what, undercover charity?"

"Something like that."

Dawn studied his profile as they walked. There was more to the story; there was always more to Thomas's stories, but she could sense the truth beneath the careful editing. "Very Clark Kent of you."

"I don't think I could pull off the glasses."

"You'd need the curl. The hair curl is very important to the whole Superman look."

"I'll work on that."

They'd reached the town square, where the enormous Christmas tree dominated the center like a glittering monument to holiday excess. White lights outlined every branch, and tinsel caught the streetlights like captured starlight.

Thomas stopped walking. "This is nice," he said, looking up at the tree.

Dawn followed his gaze, but somehow she sensed he wasn't just referring to the tree. He was talking about the moment, standing here together in the snow-covered square, holding folders full of shared responsibilities, having a conversation that felt easy and natural despite barely knowing each other.

"I'm glad we're doing this together," he said.

The words were simple, but something in his tone made Dawn's chest tighten. When she looked at him, his guard had lowered a bit. He seemed younger, less cautious—more like someone who wanted to be here rather than someone tangled in complicated circumstances.

Snow started to fall, the soft, chunky flakes making everything seem like a Christmas card. Thomas tilted his face up to catch a few snowflakes, and Dawn watched him with the strange feeling of recognizing someone even though they'd just met.

The moment stretched between them, warm despite the cold air, until Dawn forced herself to step back.

"I should get home," she said. "Family dinner waits for no one, especially when you've just volunteered for major community responsibilities."

"Right. Of course." Thomas nodded, a flash of something passing across his face too quickly to interpret. "I'll see you tomorrow? We should probably start planning."

"Tomorrow at 10 AM? We can meet at the community center."

"It's a date." He paused, seeming to realize what he'd said. "I mean, an appointment. A planning meeting. Very professional."

Dawn found herself smiling despite her best efforts to keep a proper co-chair distance. "Very professional," she agreed.

She walked home through the falling snow, her gala folder tucked under her arm, thinking about how Thomas had looked at the Christmas tree. About the fact that she'd committed to weeks of working closely with someone she found increasingly interesting. About the way he'd said "I'm glad we're doing this together" like he meant more than just event planning.

By the time she arrived at her parents' house, she had realized two things: First, she had just agreed to be responsible for Holly Falls' biggest social event of the year, which was either the worst decision she had made in months or exactly the kind of local commitment that proved she was serious about staying.

Second, she was more excited about tomorrow's planning meeting than she had been about anything in a long time.

Which was probably something she should be worried about, but she found herself smiling anyway.

At home, Amy was waiting in the kitchen with two cups of hot chocolate and the expression of someone who had questions.

"So," Amy said, sliding a mug across the table. "Thomas Miller seems nice."

"He seems helpful. Very organized. Good with logistics."

"Uh-huh." Amy sipped her hot chocolate. "And handsome."

"I hadn't noticed."

"Dawn."

"Okay, fine. Objectively handsome. But we're co-chairs. It's purely professional."

Amy's laugh was entirely too knowing. "Right. Professional. That's why you're glowing."

"I'm not glowing. I'm cold from walking home."

"You're definitely glowing." Amy leaned back in her chair, looking satisfied. "This is going to be interesting."

Dawn thought about Thomas standing under the Christmas tree, snowflakes in his hair, saying he was glad they were doing this together. About the way her stomach had flipped when he'd called their planning meeting a date, even though he'd immediately corrected himself.

"Yeah," she said, taking a sip of her hot chocolate. "It really is."

Later that night, buried beneath flannel sheets that had long since lost their lavender scent, Dawn stared at the cracked ceiling as if it might hold answers. The wind moaned outside, dragging icy fingers across the windowpane, but her thoughts remained warm, dangerously so.

Thomas.

That ridiculous grin still flickered behind his eyes, the one he'd flashed after she accidentally smeared whipped cream across his brow while wrestling with the rogue garland that wouldn't stay up. He hadn't flinched, hadn't cursed. Just laughed—rich, unfiltered—and wiped the mess away with the back of his hand like he'd done it a hundred times before. Then he looked at her, truly looked at her, and that smile softened. It sank into his jaw, traced the sharp line of his cheekbones, and settled into something that made her stomach shift uncomfortably under the blankets.

She turned over, pressed her face into the pillow, and groaned.

She was going to have to work with him again. Tomorrow. Maybe all week. The decorating project wasn't finished, not even close, and she'd agreed, foolishly, to "team up" until the storefront looked like Christmas had exploded in a burst of color. There'd be more tinsel. More coffee runs. More of that lopsided charm he wore like armor, hiding whatever scars she didn't have the right to name.

Dawn clutched the edge of the blanket and told herself, firmly, that she could keep her distance. She'd done it before, with men who smiled too easily and made promises with their eyes. This would be no different. It had to be no different.

Getting close wasn't just risky.

It was a form of suicide. Emotional, professional, maybe even spiritual. She didn't have space in her life for messy entanglements or spark-eyed optimists with steady hands and inconvenient dimples.

She closed her eyes, heart tapping a warning rhythm against her ribs.

Tomorrow, she'd staple garland and hang fake snowflakes and pretend his laugh didn't echo in the back of her mind.

And when he smiled again, because he likely would, she'd smile back. Politely. From a distance. Far enough so she couldn't smell the cedar and coffee on his coat. Far enough that she wouldn't start hoping he might stay.

Chapter 5:
The Flight Risk

Dawn had been staring at her phone for an hour. It was before dawn, and she was wide awake in her bedroom, thumb hovering over the airline app she'd downloaded earlier, when sleep became impossible and staying in Holly Falls started to feel suffocating.

There were flights leaving from Indianapolis. Several options. She could be on the 6 AM flight to Austin, returning to familiar territory where no one expected her to co-chair anything or make commitments that lasted longer than a coffee break. Or she could catch the 8:15 to Portland, where the weather was consistently terrible, and no one would ask about Christmas plans. Alternatively, she might choose the 10:30 to anywhere else, because elsewhere had the clear benefit of not being here.

This was her way of acting. This defined who she was. She stayed until staying became dangerous, then she left before leaving became hard. It wasn't fleeing; it was strategic repositioning. It was smart.

Her suitcase sat in the corner of the room, still mostly packed. She never fully unpacked anywhere. Old habit, carefully maintained. You couldn't make a quick exit if you'd scattered your belongings like breadcrumbs through someone else's life.

Dawn opened the booking app, cursor blinking at her like an invitation to freedom. She typed in tomorrow's date. Destination: anywhere but Holly Falls, Indiana, population 8,000, known for its aggressive Christmas cheer and gala co-chair assignments that felt suspiciously like commitment.

But before she could hit search, her phone buzzed.

A message from Thomas, sent late, probably when he returned to where he's staying: *Thanks for not throwing any drinks at me today. Progress. See you tomorrow, I have ideas for the gala. Fair warning: some of them are bad.*

Dawn stared at the message. Read it once. Twice. Three times.

It was nothing. A joke. The kind of casual text you send to someone you barely know, filled with simple humor and the belief that tomorrow would go as planned.

See you tomorrow, I have ideas.

He was assuming she would be there. He expected her presence as a certainty, as if she were the kind of person who always showed up when she said she would.

Dawn put the phone down. Picked it up. Read the messages again.

She should correct that assumption. Should book the flight, send something vague about plans changing, and disappear the way she always did. Clean. Simple. No one got hurt because no one got close enough to hurt.

Instead, she closed the airline app and lay back down, phone on her chest, staring at the glow-in-the-dark stars she'd stuck to the ceiling when she was twelve. They still faintly glowed in the darkness, plastic constellations that had outlived her childhood, her adolescence, and every version of herself that had fled this room.

She wasn't staying because Amy guilt-tripped her. She wasn't staying due to family obligations, Christmas traditions, or the mayor's enthusiastic clipboard management.

She might be staying because she wanted to hear Thomas's bad ideas.

That was terrifying.

Dawn lay awake until it was morning, watching her childhood stars fade as the light grew brighter, and wondered what was wrong with her that she was staying somewhere that made her feel like she might want to belong.

By morning, she was worn out and determined to act as if the previous night's crisis had never occurred.

She came downstairs late to find Amy at the kitchen table with coffee and what looked like seventeen different folders related to festival planning.

"You look terrible," Amy said without looking up from her clipboard. "Did you sleep?"

"Define sleep."

"Unconsciousness lasting more than twenty minutes."

"Then no."

Amy slides a coffee mug across the table. "Rough night?"

Dawn sat down, wrapped her hands around the mug, and considered lying. Decided she was too tired to be creative.

"I almost booked a flight."

Amy's pen quit moving. She looked up, her expression carefully neutral. "And?"

"I didn't."

"What stopped you?"

Dawn pondered the message. About bad ideas and the hope for tomorrow. About how Thomas looked at the Christmas tree as if he was seeing magic instead of just holiday decorations.

"I don't know," she said, which was a lie. But some truths felt too fragile to hand over, even to Amy.

Amy was silent for a moment, studying Dawn with the focused attention she usually reserved for budget spreadsheets. "You know I'm not going to tell you to stay," she said finally. "That's not my job."

"Could've fooled me with yesterday's volunteer ambush."

"That was sisterly manipulation. Completely different." Amy's mouth quirked in what might have been a smile. "But the rest of it, whether you leave, how long you stay, what you do with your time here, that's yours. I just don't want you to run because you're scared of wanting something."

The words landed with the uncomfortable accuracy of someone who'd known you for thirty years and recognized your patterns better than you did.

"I'm not scared," Dawn said, unconvincing even to herself.

"Sure you're not." Amy said, standing and quickly gathering her festival folders. "I'm meeting Will for lunch. There's more coffee, and Thomas texted to ask about vendor permits, so apparently he's taking this gala thing seriously."

After Amy left, Dawn sat alone in the kitchen with her coffee and the quiet knowledge that she wasn't leaving today. She also knew she wouldn't be leaving tomorrow either.

She might be in trouble.

Her phone buzzed mid-afternoon as she halfheartedly sketched design ideas for the gala decorations. Thomas, as promised:

Want to help set up for the Holiday Market? I've been volunteered by someone named Edna to assist with booth construction. She seems to think I need supervision.

Dawn looked at the message. She should say no. Maintain professional distance, focus on their co-chair duties, and avoid any activities that seem suspiciously like hanging out.

She typed back: *Where and when?*

The Holiday Market was Holly Falls' weekly gathering for the community, turning into a display of competitive Christmas spirit in December. Local vendors set up booths around the town square, selling everything from handmade crafts to dubious fudge, while children ran circles around their parents and teenagers acted too cool for the obvious charm.

Dawn found Thomas near the gazebo, looking somewhat overwhelmed while a lively woman directed his efforts to assemble what looked like a pie display.

"You're holding it wrong," Edna Morrison informed him, hands on her hips. "The support beam goes in the slot, not on top of the slot."

"I'm not sure there is a slot," Thomas said diplomatically.

"There's always a slot. You just have to find it."

Dawn approached cautiously. "Need backup?"

Thomas looked up with an expression of profound relief. "Please. I'm apparently failing at booth architecture."

Edna noticed Dawn and instantly lit up. "Perfect! You can help him figure out this nonsense while I grab the pies from Marv." She hurried away, leaving Dawn and Thomas staring at an instruction manual that looked like it was written in hieroglyphics.

"How long have you two been dating?" Edna called over her shoulder.

"We're not—" Dawn started.

"We met three days ago," Thomas added.

"Marv and I got engaged after three weeks," Edna said cheerfully. "When you know, you know."

She vanished into the crowd, leaving Dawn and Thomas in the awkward silence that followed well-meaning small-town assumptions.

"Sorry," Thomas said. "She's been treating us like a couple since I arrived. I think it's because we were both standing near her booth at the same time."

"Small towns," Dawn said. "Everyone's a matchmaker."

They worked on the booth assembly in quiet comfort, with Dawn translating the instructions while Thomas handled the construction skills she lacked. It was easy work, the kind that filled time without needing conversation, though Dawn remained aware of his proximity every time he reached past her for tools or adjusted the booth frame.

"You're good at this," she observed as he managed to make sense of the structural engineering that had baffled both her and Edna.

"Basic construction. I've done some building projects."

"What kind of projects?"

The pause was quick but evident. "Community centers. Libraries. Public space improvements."

True but cautious, Dawn noted. Thomas had a way of answering questions without fully answering, giving facts that seemed complete until you realized what was absent.

By evening, the market had transformed. White lights strung between trees cast everything in a warm gold glow, and the smell of mulled cider mixed with kettle corn and the sweet aroma of too many Christmas cookies. Children ran between booths while teenagers gathered near the hot chocolate stand, and families wandered slowly through the organized chaos.

Dawn found herself narrating the town for Thomas, pointing out vendors she had known since childhood and sharing stories about how the market had changed over the years. She talked about Holly Falls as if she loved it, even though she'd spent a decade insisting she couldn't wait to leave.

Mrs. Patterson has been selling the same seven cookie varieties for fifteen years, "Dawn said as they passed a booth decorated with an overly festive amount of holly. "The secret ingredient in her snickerdoodles is actually cardamom, but she'll deny it if you ask."

"Trade secrets are sacred," Thomas agreed solemnly.

"And see that booth with all the woodwork? That's Mr. Mathews. He retired from engineering and started making architecturally perfect birdhouses. I think he misses having blueprints to follow."

Thomas listened with the focused attention of someone genuinely interested in the social dynamics of a place he was still learning. "You know everyone."

"Small town. Whether you want to or not."

"Is that good or bad?"

Dawn considered. "Both. It's like living in a fishbowl, but it's a fishbowl where people notice if you're gone and care if you're hurt." She paused. "I forgot that, I think. The caring part."

They stopped near the center of the square where carnival games had been set up, such as ring toss, basketball hoops, and a duck pond that was definitely rigged. Thomas examined the game booths with an expression of someone who'd never encountered anything so wonderfully ridiculous.

"Have you never been to a carnival?" Dawn asked.

"Not really. Charity galas, yes. Ring toss, no."

"That's tragic. Everyone should have the experience of losing money to obviously rigged games."

"Is that what we're doing?"

"Absolutely."

Dawn guided him through ring toss with the patience of someone who had grown up attending these markets. Thomas was terrible at it, which somehow made watching him try even more amusing. He approached each throw with scientific precision, adjusting his stance and calculating angles as if he were planning a military operation.

"You're overthinking it," Dawn told him after his fourth consecutive miss.

"I don't overthink things."

"You just spent thirty seconds analyzing the aerodynamics of a plastic ring."

"That was efficiency analysis."

On his seventh attempt, Thomas finally managed to land a ring around a bottle. His genuine expression of triumph made Dawn laugh out loud, and he grinned back at her.

"What did I win?" he asked the booth operator.

"Take your pick from the prize wall."

Thomas examined the options, which included stuffed animals that ranged from adorable to vaguely unsettling, and chose the most crazed-looking reindeer Dawn had ever seen. It was brown and lumpy, with eyes that hinted at either deep wisdom or utter madness.

"This one," he said, presenting it to Dawn with ceremony. "You're my coach. Coaches deserve tribute."

Dawn took the reindeer, which was even more unsettling up close. "What should I name it?"

"Harold."

"Harold?"

"He looks like a Harold."

Dawn studied Harold's unhinged expression. "He absolutely does."

They were walking past the gazebo when the sound of caroling reached them, a group of teenagers and adults gathered near the Christmas tree, attempting "Silent Night" with more enthusiasm than accuracy.

Thomas stopped walking. "They sound..."

"Terrible?" Dawn suggested.

"Joyful."

Before Dawn could stop him, Thomas had joined the group, adding his voice to the chorus. He was terrible, completely tone-deaf and enthusiastic about it, but somehow that made it more charming rather than worse.

Dawn stood on the edge of the group, clutching Harold and watching Thomas murder "Silent Night" with genuine happiness, and something in her chest loosened. Before she could talk herself out of it, she stepped forward and added her own voice to the chaos.

They were both awful. The song was a wreck. Dawn couldn't remember the last time she had felt so carefree and happy.

When the caroling turned into laughter and hot chocolate suggestions, Thomas fell into step beside Dawn as they headed toward the edge of the square.

"Thank you," he said.

"For what?"

"Today. This." He gestured toward the market, the lights, and the overall feeling of organized Christmas chaos. "I haven't done anything like this in years."

"Carnival games and terrible caroling?"

"Fun. I haven't had fun in a while."

There was something in his voice that made Dawn look at him more closely. In the light of the Christmas tree, he seemed younger somehow. Less guarded, like someone who had forgotten what it felt like to be somewhere just because he wanted to be there.

They reached the edge of the square where the crowd thinned, and the noise fell to a distant hum. Thomas's hand brushed hers as they walked, and instead of pulling away, Dawn let him hold it. His fingers were warm despite the cold air, and holding his hand felt the most natural thing in the world.

At her front door, they halted. Dawn realized she wasn't ready for the evening to end, which was risky for someone who specialized in strategic exits.

"I almost left today," she said, surprising herself with the admission.

Thomas turned to face her fully. "But you didn't."

"I didn't."

"Why?"

Dawn thought about the early morning crisis, the airline app, and the text that prevented her from booking a flight to anywhere else. She thought about how he'd assumed she'd be there tomorrow, as if her presence was something to plan around.

"You said you had bad ideas," she said. "I wanted to hear them."

Thomas smiled, and it was the kind of smile that reached his eyes. "They're really terrible ideas."

"I can handle terrible."

"Good," he said. "Because I'm pretty sure planning this gala with me is going to be the worst decision you've made in weeks."

"I've made many questionable decisions recently. It will have competition."

"I'll try to earn the title."

Dawn went inside, Harold tucked under her arm, and stood in the front hallway, listening to Thomas's footsteps fade down the street. She stayed. Not because anyone asked her to, not out of guilt or obligation, but because she wanted to.

She climbed the stairs to her childhood bedroom, set Harold on the dresser where his wild eyes could watch over the room, and confessed to herself what she had been avoiding all day:

She was in trouble.

Not the kind of trouble she could fix by leaving town, changing her phone number, or pretending nothing had happened. The kind of trouble that comes from wanting something or someone enough to take the risk of staying in one place long enough to see what might grow.

Harold stared at her with his demented reindeer wisdom, and Dawn stared back.

"Don't look at me like that," she told him. "I know what I'm doing."

Harold's expression suggested he had opinions about that claim.

Dawn turned off the light and lay down in her childhood bed, listening to Holly Falls settle into evening quiet around her. Tomorrow, she'd have to face whatever comes next, more gala planning, more time with Thomas, more chances to make choices that felt like building instead of running.

But tonight, she was here. She'd chosen to be here.

For now, that felt like enough.

Chapter 6:
The Mistletoe Mess

Merry Materials was Holly Falls' only craft store, and Dolores Manning had been running it for thirty-seven years with the iron determination of someone who believed strongly in both customer service and quality control.

"Glitter is a commitment," she informed Dawn and Thomas as they walked through the door that morning. "You don't use glitter unless you're prepared to find it in your hair for the next six months. And in your car. And possibly your underclothes."

Dawn had called ahead to reserve workspace, which in a town this size meant Dolores had moved three bolts of fabric off a table near the back and declared it theirs for the morning. Thomas followed behind Dawn with coffee and the increasingly thick folder of gala planning materials, looking like someone who'd never been inside a craft store and wasn't entirely sure about the experience.

"Have you ever made decorations before?" Dawn asked as she spread fabric swatches across their commandeered table.

"Define 'made.'"

"Personally created with your own hands. Not supervised. Not delegated. Actually made."

Thomas considered this. "Then no."

Dawn paused in arranging ribbon samples. "Not even in school? Art class? Summer camp?"

"I went to the kind of school where they had art appreciation, not art making. And summer camp was more about networking than crafts."

There was something carefully neutral about the way he said it, like he was describing someone else's life. Dawn filed it away with the other small mysteries that seemed to accumulate around Thomas Miller, the expensive watch, the careful answers, the way he approached manual tasks like they were puzzles he'd never seen before.

"Well," she said, holding up two ribbons. "Today you learn. Velvet or satin for the centerpieces?"

Thomas studied the ribbons with the focused attention most people reserved for major life decisions. "What's the theme again?"

"Winter night. Deep blues, silver, touches of white. I want elegant but not stuffy. Magical but not ridiculous."

"The velvet," he said after a moment. "It'll catch the light better under whatever lighting system the community center has, and it won't look cheap if we have to stretch the budget."

Dawn looked at him with surprise. "That's actually a very good point."

"I may not make things, but I've been to enough events to know what works." He paused. "My family was involved in a lot of charity functions. You learn to notice what makes people feel comfortable versus what just looks expensive."

Another careful half-truth. Dawn was beginning to recognize his pattern; everything he said was technically accurate, but it felt like he was translating from a language she didn't speak.

"Okay," she said, setting the velvet aside. "Velvet it is. Now for the actual making part."

Dawn had planned centerpieces that would work with the community center's limited resources: wire-wrapped pinecones and branches arranged in simple glass bowls with battery-operated string lights. Elegant, affordable, and theoretically foolproof.

She demonstrated the technique on the first pinecone, wrapping the wire around the base, twisting to secure, and leaving a long tail for arrangement flexibility. Simple. Basic. Something you could teach a reasonably coordinated ten-year-old.

Thomas watched intently, then picked up a pinecone and a length of wire.

His first attempt looked like the pinecone had been attacked.

"How," Dawn asked, staring at the mangled result, "did you manage to make it look angry?"

"I may have been too forceful with the initial wrap."

Thomas's second attempt crushed half the pinecone's scales. His third somehow resulted in him cutting his finger on a wire that shouldn't have been sharp enough to cut anything.

"This is unprecedented," Dawn said, watching him suck on his injured finger while glaring at the offending pinecone. "I've never seen anyone lose a fight with a pinecone before."

"I have a theory that craft supplies are sentient and hostile."

"Or," Dawn suggested, "you're overthinking it."

She moved closer, taking the wire from his hands. "You're gripping too hard. Let the tool do the work."

Standing beside him, she could smell his soap, something clean and expensive that probably cost more than her monthly coffee budget. She was aware of his proximity, the way he held very still as she positioned his hands on the wire.

"Like this," she said, covering his hands with hers. "Just gentle pressure. Guide it, don't force it."

His hands were warm under hers. Steady. There were calluses on his palms that surprised her, not the soft hands of someone who'd never done physical work, but not the hands of someone who did it regularly either.

"Now twist," she said, her voice coming out quieter than she'd intended.

Thomas made the motion, and this time it worked. The wire wrapped neatly around the pinecone base, secure but not crushing.

"I did it." He sounded genuinely pleased, more pleased than the accomplishment warranted. "That's my best work."

"It's your fourth pinecone."

"My best fourth pinecone."

Dawn realized she was still holding his hands. His fingers were warm under hers, and he'd gone very still. She could feel his breath catch slightly.

She should step back. This was supposed to be a work session, not whatever this was becoming.

But she didn't step back. Instead, she found herself studying his profile, the way his dark hair fell across his forehead, the small scar near his left eye that she hadn't noticed before.

"You're a quick learner," she said finally.

"I have a good teacher."

The moment stretched between them, charged with something Dawn wasn't ready to name. Behind them, she could hear Dolores humming as she arranged yarn displays, but it felt distant, as if they were in their own pocket of space.

Finally, Dawn stepped back, clearing her throat. "Okay. You're on pinecone duty. I'll handle the ribbon work. Division of labor."

"Understood." Thomas's voice was carefully neutral, but there was something in his eyes, awareness, maybe, or the same uncertainty Dawn was feeling.

They worked in companionable quiet for the next hour. Dawn fell into her creative rhythm, cutting ribbon lengths and testing arrangements while Thomas improved marginally with the pinecones. His technique was still awkward, but he approached each one with methodical patience that was oddly endearing.

At some point, his phone buzzed on the table. He reached for it automatically, and Dawn caught a glimpse of the lock screen before he turned it away.

It was a photo of a building, modern, glass-walled, impressively tall. Not a personal photo, no people or pets. Just architecture.

"What's that?" Dawn asked, curiosity winning over politeness.

Thomas glanced at his phone, then locked it quickly. "Nothing. Just... a project I was working on."

"A building?"

"Sort of. My family's in development. Real estate stuff." He said it casually, but Dawn caught the slight deflection again, the way he never quite answered directly.

"Development," she repeated, filing this new information away with the rest of his careful non-answers. "That's a big change from consulting."

"It's all connected. Strategy, development, problem-solving." Thomas held up his latest pinecone, which was lopsided but functional. "Boring stuff. Nothing like this."

"You're saying pinecones are more satisfying than real estate development?"

"I'm saying making something with your hands is satisfying. Even badly." He studied his handiwork. "This exists because I made it exist. That's... rare. For me."

There was something vulnerable in the admission, a glimpse of something real underneath his careful pleasantness. Dawn heard it and wanted to ask more, but before she could, Dolores appeared at their table.

"How are we doing over here?" she asked, surveying their progress with the critical eye of someone who'd seen a lot of craft disasters. "Oh, these are lovely. Very elegant. Much better than the Henderson twins' attempt last year, they used so much glitter I'm still finding it in the carpet."

"Glitter is a commitment," Dawn said solemnly.

"Exactly. You understand." Dolores beamed at them. "You two make a good team. Very complementary skills."

Dawn felt her cheeks warm. "We're just partners for the gala."

"Of course you are, dear." Dolores's tone suggested she had opinions about that classification but was too polite to share them directly.

By noon, they'd made enough centerpiece components for a dozen tables and Dawn's hands were cramping from wire work. Thomas suggested lunch, and before Dawn could suggest somewhere safely public, he was leading her toward Pine & Dine with the confidence of someone who'd clearly scouted the local dining options.

The diner was exactly what Dawn remembered, red vinyl booths, checkered floors, a menu that hadn't changed since 1987, and enough local characters to populate a small soap opera. Their arrival was noted immediately.

Marge, the waitress who'd been working there since Dawn was in high school, appeared at their table with coffee and the expression of someone conducting reconnaissance.

"Dawn Donovan," she said warmly. "Good to see you, honey. And this must be our mysterious volunteer."

"Thomas Miller," Thomas said, extending his hand. "Nice to meet you."

"Miller," Marge repeated, like she was filing it away for later analysis. "You're not from around here."

"No, ma'am. Just visiting for the holidays."

"Visiting from where?"

Dawn watched Thomas navigate the interrogation with practiced charm, deflecting personal questions while somehow making everyone feel like he was being forthcoming. He mentioned appreciating small towns, enjoying the community spirit, and looking forward to the holiday celebrations. All true, all completely uninformative.

By the time they finished lunch, they'd been visited by Hank from the hardware store (who wanted to know if Thomas was handy with tools), Eleanor from the jewelry shop (who thought he looked familiar), and Mrs. Patterson (who asked directly if he was single and available for her niece).

Thomas handled each interaction with the same friendly evasiveness, never quite giving a complete answer, never mentioning where he was staying or how long he'd be in town.

"You're good at that," Dawn observed as they walked back toward the town square.

"At what?"

"Answering questions without actually answering them."

Thomas was quiet for a moment. "Small towns ask a lot of questions."

"Only because they care. It's not malicious."

"I know that. I just..." He paused, seeming to choose his words carefully. "I value privacy. Some things aren't anyone else's business."

Dawn nodded, understanding the impulse even as she wondered what he was so careful not to reveal. "Fair enough. We all have things we'd rather keep to ourselves."

They'd arrived at the town square, where the huge Christmas tree dominated the center like a glittering monument to holiday cheer. The Wishing Fountain sat close by, its small pool mirroring the gray December sky.

"Can I ask you something?" Thomas said, stopping near the fountain.

"Sure."

"What would you wish for? If you were going to make a wish here."

The question took Dawn by surprise. She thought about the wish she'd already made, tucked inside Nana's ornament, *a place to land, someone who won't make her stay*, and felt her chest tighten.

"I don't know," she said. "World peace? An end to poverty? The usual beauty pageant answers."

"Those aren't wishes. Those are noble goals." Thomas's eyes were serious. "I mean something personal. Something just for you."

Dawn gazed at the fountain, watching the coins scattered at the bottom left by other wishers with different hopes. "I don't really do personal wishes."

"Why not?"

"Because wanting something specific is dangerous. You might get it, or you might not get it, and either way you're disappointed."

Thomas considered this. "What if I proposed a bet?"

"What kind of bet?"

"The raffle tickets for the gala. Whoever sells more by Saturday gets bragging rights."

Dawn raised an eyebrow. "And the loser?"

"Has to make a wish. Here. At the Wishing Fountain. Out loud. In public."

Dawn's stomach flipped. The idea of speaking her real wish, or any wish, in front of Thomas felt impossible. "That's not much of a consequence."

"It is if you're someone who doesn't do personal wishes."

She should say no. Should deflect with humor, change the subject, or find some other way to avoid precisely the kind of emotional vulnerability the bet would require.

Instead, she found herself nodding. "Fine. You're on."

They shook hands. Thomas's grip was warm and firm, and he held on a beat too long before letting go.

"You're not going to know what I'd wish for," Dawn said. "Because I'm going to win."

"That's the spirit."

Walking home, Dawn realized she had just committed to a competition where losing meant exposing herself publicly, and winning meant avoiding the opportunity to speak up about something she genuinely cared about.

Either way, she was in trouble.

That night, Dawn lay in bed with Harold the Reindeer leaning against her pillow, his slightly unhinged eyes reflecting the glow from her bedside lamp.

"Don't look at me like that," she told him. "I know what I'm doing."

Harold's expression suggested he had opinions about that claim, none of them flattering.

Dawn thought about the day, the craft store, the teaching moment, and the warmth of Thomas's hands under hers. She thought about his thoughtful answers and the building on his phone, as well as how he never quite told the whole truth about anything.

He was hiding something. She was sure of that now. She just didn't know what, or if it mattered.

And the thing was, she was hiding too. Her fear, her flight patterns, the wish she'd already made that she didn't fully understand.

Maybe that's why they worked well together. Two people hiding parts of themselves, finding connection in the spaces between secrets.

Or maybe that's why this was dangerous.

Dawn turned off the light and settled into bed, listening as Holly Falls quieted around her. In the darkness, she could still feel the echo of Thomas's hands in hers, warm, unfamiliar, and starting to feel like something she could get used to.

That was the scariest part of all.

Chapter 7:
Tangled Up in You

D awn was eating breakfast when Amy made the announcement that would change the trajectory of her entire day.

"Thomas is coming to the tree farm."

Dawn choked on her toast. "What?"

"I invited him. He said yes." Amy buttered her own toast with casual aggression, a telltale sign that she had done something Dawn wouldn't approve of. "It's a family tradition. He's helping with the gala. He's basically family by default for now."

"He's a stranger."

"He's a stranger you've spent the last four days with. And made pinecones with. And went caroling with."

Dawn's stomach dropped. "How do you know about the caroling?"

"Edna texted Mom. Mom texted me. Holly Falls is a small town, Dawn. Nothing is secret, you know that." Amy took a deliberate bite of toast. "Besides, I think it'll be good for him."

"Good for him, how?"

"He seems lonely. Like someone who hasn't had a proper Christmas in a while."

Dawn processed this. Thomas, at the tree farm. With her family. In the context where she wasn't "Dawn who's helping with the gala" but "Dawn, daughter, sister, person with a childhood and embarrassing stories and a bedroom still decorated with glow-in-the-dark stars."

"This is a terrible idea."

"It's a great idea. Eat your toast. We leave in an hour."

An hour later, Dawn found herself in the back of her parents' car, listening to her mother explain the family tree selection criteria to Will, who was riding shotgun because he'd been promoted to official "family" status somewhere around the engagement.

"The key is proportion," Patricia was saying. "Height matters, but so does fullness. Last year, we got a tree that looked perfect in the lot but had a dead spot in the back that we didn't discover until we got it home."

"Like dating," Will said mildly, which made Amy laugh and Doug snort from the driver's seat.

Dawn watched the familiar countryside roll by and tried to prepare herself for whatever strange things were about to happen. Thomas, becoming part of her family's most sacred tradition. Thomas, meeting her parents not as a casual stranger but as someone Amy had specifically invited into their inner circle.

The Holly Falls Tree Farm was a twenty-minute drive from town, run by the Bergstrom family since 1952. It was vividly charming in the way small-town Christmas scenes tend to be: snow-covered pines lined up perfectly, a red barn decorated with garland, a hand-painted sign offering free hot chocolate and the promise of "Christmas Magic Every Day!"

Thomas was already there when they arrived.

He'd driven separately, staying at the inn meant he had his own transportation, which Dawn noted was a rental car nice enough to be slightly out of place among the farm trucks and family SUVs in the gravel lot.

"You made it," Dawn said, getting out of her parents' car.

"I was invited. It seemed rude to decline," Thomas smiled, and Dawn realized he was nervous. Actually nervous. It was the first time she'd seen him anything other than entirely composed.

"Amy doesn't give people the option to decline."

"I noticed." His smile widened. "Your sister is... formidable."

"That's one word for it."

Before Dawn could warn him about what was coming, her parents descended on Thomas with the eagerness of people who had heard news. Her mother hugged him, truly hugged him, which she didn't do with strangers, and her father extended his hand for what Dawn recognized as the official Doug Donovan Assessment Handshake.

"So you're the young man keeping my daughter out of trouble," Doug said, applying what looked like a significant amount of pressure.

"I think she's keeping me out of trouble, sir."

"Smart answer." Doug clapped him on the shoulder, apparently satisfied with whatever the handshake had communicated. "Let's go find a tree."

The Donovan family's approach to choosing a Christmas tree was deliberate. Patricia had established standards after thirty years of selecting trees. The tree needed to be full, symmetrical, stand between seven and eight feet tall, have few bare spots, and a shape that would fit their specific ornament collection. She had turned down trees for reasons Dawn still didn't fully grasp, using terms like "needle retention" and "branch spacing."

They spread out among the rows of Fraser firs, each family member taking responsibility for scouting different sections. Dawn found herself walking with Thomas while her parents moved ahead, with Amy and Will trailing behind them in the comfortable silence of people who had been together long enough to communicate without words.

"Your family is nice," Thomas said, his breath forming small clouds in the cold air.

"They're interrogating you. That's different from nice."

"It's a nice interrogation. Very warm."

"My dad did the handshake thing. The grip test."

"I noticed. Do you think I passed?"

"You're still here, so probably." Dawn glanced at him sideways. He was studying her parents, who were currently engaged in what appeared to be a serious discussion about the merits of a particular tree. "You look like you've never seen a family pick out a Christmas tree before."

Thomas was quiet for a moment. "This is different," he said finally.

"Different from what?"

"From how I grew up. Christmas was..." He paused, choosing his words with the same careful precision she'd noticed before. "Formal. Events. Schedules. Not..." He gestured toward her parents, who were now debating branch density with the intensity of contract negotiations. "Not this."

Dawn watched him watch her family, and she caught something hungry in his expression. Something lonely that made her chest feel tight.

"It's not always this wholesome," she said. "Last year, my dad got the tree stuck in the car door, and we had to drive home with the trunk open. Amy cried. There was eggnog involved."

Thomas laughed, but it was soft, as if he were afraid to make too much noise. "That sounds perfect, actually."

"It was a disaster."

"Perfect disasters." He looked at her, and something in his eyes made Dawn want to ask questions she wasn't sure she was ready to have answered. "The best kind."

They were interrupted by Patricia's triumphant call from several rows away. She had found The Tree, a tall, full Fraser fir meeting all the criteria. Doug went to the barn to get the saw, but before he could return, Dawn stepped forward.

"I'll do it," she said.

Everyone looked at her.

"You'll do what?" Patricia asked.

"Cut it down. I can cut down a tree."

"Have you ever cut down a tree?" Amy asked, her tone suggesting she already knew the answer.

"How hard can it be? Saw goes back and forth. The tree falls. Done."

Doug returned with the saw, his expression carefully neutral, the expression of a father who has learned not to argue with his daughters about competence, especially when those daughters are thirty and fully capable of making their own mistakes.

Dawn took the saw, knelt in the snow at the base of the tree, and started cutting.

She quickly discovered that cutting down a tree was significantly harder than it appeared in movies.

The saw kept catching. Her arm position was wrong. The angle wasn't right. After thirty seconds, her arms were burning, and she'd made what appeared to be very little progress. She was acutely aware of everyone watching—Thomas especially—and that awareness made her more determined to prove she could handle this on her own.

"Do you want help?" Thomas asked gently.

"No."

"I could hold the branches back—"

"I've got it."

She didn't have it. But she was committed now, and Dawn Donovan didn't quit things just because they were harder than expected. The saw bit deeper into the trunk. The tree creaked ominously.

"Dawn," Thomas said, his voice suddenly sharp with alarm. "Move."

She looked up from her work and saw the tree starting to fall. Not away from her, as physics and common sense indicated it should, but sideways, toward her, because apparently she had angled the cut wrong, which was something that can happen when you've never cut down a tree before and are too stubborn to accept help.

Thomas grabbed her arm and yanked her backward just as the tree crashed down right where she had been kneeling, with branches thrashing and snow exploding all around.

They tumbled backward together, landing hard in a snowbank behind them, Dawn on her back with Thomas half on top of her, both of them covered in snow and pine needles.

For a moment, neither of them moved. This was the moment in romantic comedies when eyes locked, breath caught, and romantic tension swelled, snow sparkling around them like nature's confetti. But instead:

"Ow," Dawn said.

"Are you okay?" Thomas asked, trying to push himself up.

"You're on my hair."

"Sorry—" He shifted, and she yelped.

"That's my hand you're crushing."

"I'm trying to—"

They were both struggling now, tangled in each other and the snowbank, making everything worse. Every time one of them tried to move, they destabilized the other. Dawn got a face full of snow when Thomas tried to roll off her. Thomas's elbow hit something solid, making him grunt in pain.

"This is the least romantic moment of my life," Dawn said, spitting snow.

"I was going to say the same thing."

"Should we help?" Amy called from somewhere nearby, her voice carefully controlled in a way that suggested she was trying not to laugh.

"NO!" both Dawn and Thomas said simultaneously.

It took another full minute of awkward maneuvering before they managed to free themselves from the snowbank and each other. Dawn stood up, brushing snow out of her hair, and assessed the damage. Thomas had pine needles stuck to his coat and snow in his hair, and there would be a bruise on her hip tomorrow, but they were both okay.

"Well," Doug said, surveying the fallen tree, which was lying exactly where it should be despite Dawn's unconventional approach to timber felling. "That's one way to do it."

"The tree is fine," Patricia added helpfully. "Just needs to settle."

Dawn looked at Thomas, still pulling needles out of his hair. "Thank you," she whispered. "For the tackle. I would have been a pancake."

"You would have been fine," Thomas said, but his voice was tense in a way that showed he'd really been scared for her.

They loaded the tree onto the car, with Doug and Will doing most of the work while Thomas helped and Dawn supervised from a safe distance, then drove home with the windows cracked to let the pine scent fill the car.

Back at the house, the tree decorating continued in line with thirty years of family tradition. Doug wrestled the tree into the stand while Patricia directed operations from the kitchen. Amy unpacked ornaments with military efficiency, and Will stayed out of the way, offering timely compliments to prove his usefulness.

Thomas had somehow been assigned to Christmas light duty, which proved to be an overly optimistic task.

"They're tangled," he said, holding up a strand that seemed to have been part of some kind of seasonal battle.

"They're always tangled," Dawn said, taking the lights from him. "It's one of the fundamental laws of Christmas. No one knows why."

She was in the process of unknotting the lights when she noticed Thomas was wearing her father's sweatshirt. It was faded gray with "Indiana State" printed across the front in letters that had seen better decades.

"Where's your coat?" she asked.

Thomas looked down at himself. "Drying. Snow removal was more extensive than I expected." He tugged at the sweatshirt, which was a little too small across his shoulders. "Your dad loaned me this."

"The 1987 vintage. Dad's very proud of that sweatshirt."

"It's comfortable."

Dawn looked at him, truly looked. Thomas Miller sat in her family's living room, wearing her father's old college sweatshirt, holding Christmas lights he couldn't untangle, seeming like he'd been there for years instead of just hours.

He looked like he belonged.

That was dangerous thinking.

"What does your family do for Christmas?" Doug asked, settling into his chair with a mug of hot chocolate.

Thomas went very still. "We used to have formal dinners. Very scheduled. My father was particular about..." He paused, and Dawn saw his hands shake slightly as he set down an ornament. "My father passed a few years ago. Things have been different since then."

The room softened with sympathy. Patricia made a gentle sound, and Amy's expression shifted into something tender. Doug nodded as if he understood someone who had lost his father years earlier.

"I'm sorry," Patricia said. "That must be difficult, especially during the holidays."

"It is," Thomas said quietly. "This is... this is nice. Different. Better."

Dawn watched him carefully place a glass ornament on one of the lower branches, his hands steady once again. There was something raw in his voice when he talked about his father, something that hinted at grief.

Later, after the tree was decorated, the hot chocolate was finished, and Will had gone home to his own family responsibilities, Dawn walked Thomas to the door. He was still wearing her father's sweatshirt.

"I can wait," he said. "For my shirt to finish drying."

"Take the sweatshirt. Return it whenever."

"Your dad might want it back."

"That sweatshirt is from 1987. Trust me, he won't notice it's gone for a few weeks."

Thomas looked down at himself. "I look ridiculous."

"You look..." Dawn stopped. She'd been about to say something deflecting. Something safe.

Instead: "You look like you belong here."

The words lingered between them in the cold air. Thomas's expression changed, a raw and hopeful flicker crossing his face before he suppressed it.

"That's... probably the nicest thing anyone's said to me in a while."

"Don't get used to it. I'm not usually nice."

"Noted." He was smiling, but his eyes were serious. "Thank you for today. For letting me…" He gestured vaguely at the house, the warm light spilling from the windows, the life he was about to walk away from.

"For letting you get attacked by a tree and wear my dad's ugly sweatshirt?"

"Yeah." He held her gaze, smiling. "Exactly that."

After he left, Dawn stood in the doorway watching his rental car drive away down the street. Doug's sweatshirt was too small across Thomas's shoulders, but somehow, that made it better, not worse. Like he was becoming part of something instead of just visiting it.

She went inside to find Amy in the kitchen, loading the dishwasher.

"That went well," Amy said without looking up.

"Define 'well.'"

"No one got seriously hurt, Mom didn't ask about his intentions, and Dad didn't tell the story about your disastrous prom date."

"Yet," Dawn said. "Give it time."

Amy smiled, but it was gentler than her usual expression. "Can I tell you something?"

"Sure."

Amy turned to face her, holding a dish towel. "Do you know why I pushed so hard for you to come home? Really?"

Dawn sat down at the kitchen table. "Because you're bossy and you like having your way?"

"Because I missed you," Amy's voice was soft. "Because every Christmas I see you arrive and then leave, and I never know if you're coming back. And I thought…" She paused, swallowed. "I thought maybe if you had a reason to stay, something to keep you here, you might actually... stay."

Dawn's chest felt tight. "Amy—"

"I'm not trying to trap you. I know that's what you think. I just .." Amy shrugged, a small, helpless gesture. "I want my sister. For more than two weeks a year."

This wasn't Amy giving advice. It was Amy feeling vulnerable, Amy wanting something, Amy admitting that Dawn's constant leaving hurt her in ways Dawn had never fully understood.

Dawn was at a loss for words, so she did something she rarely did: she crossed the kitchen and hugged her sister.

They paused for a moment, two twins who had taken different paths, trying to find their way back to each other.

"I'm not going anywhere yet," Dawn said into Amy's shoulder.

"Promise?"

"I promise. For now."

It was the best she could offer. Amy took it.

That night, Dawn lay in bed thinking about Thomas in her father's sweatshirt, looking like he belonged in her family's living room. She thought about how his hands had shaken when he mentioned his father, and about Amy wanting her to stay. She also thought about Thomas looking at their tree as if he'd never seen one decorated with love before.

Harold the Reindeer stared at her from the dresser, his unhinged eyes offering no commentary on her increasingly complicated emotional situation.

"You're not helpful," she told him.

But as she drifted off to sleep, Dawn found herself thinking about roots and belonging, and the risky idea that staying somewhere might be worth the chance of being truly known.

Even if the person getting to know you was still a mystery himself.

Chapter 8:
Snowmen and Secrets

Amy hadn't expected that her latest engagement would land her in the middle of Holly Falls Snowman Building Contest, turns out, it's more serious than she thought.

Dawn learned this roughly thirty seconds after she arrived at the town square, when she saw Mrs. Patterson arguing with Eleanor Henley about whether pinecones counted as "natural decorating elements" or "unapproved accessories."

"There was a town hall meeting," Amy told Dawn as they signed up for the contest. "Last year, someone was disqualified for using their daughter's hair ribbons as a scarf. Apparently, there are rules about materials that are not approved ahead of time or imported."

"Imported from where?" Dawn asked, watching a man she didn't recognize measuring snow density with what appeared to be a ruler.

"Anywhere outside the immediate contest area. The stakes are low, which is why people get so intense about it."

Dawn looked around the town square, which had been turned into what could only be called a snowman building zone. Teams of two were scattered across the available space, armed with buckets, shovels, and the kind of competitive spirit usually seen at the Olympics.

"Where's Thomas?" Amy asked, consulting her clipboard. "You're signed up as a team."

"I didn't sign up as a team with anyone."

"I signed you up as part of a team. He agreed when I asked yesterday."

Dawn stared at her sister. "You asked him yesterday?"

"After decorating the tree, he seemed enthusiastic about community participation." Amy's expression was perfectly innocent, which made it her most dangerous look. "There he is."

Thomas was walking toward them across the snow-covered square, looking like someone who had prepared for an Arctic expedition rather than a small-town craft competition. He was wearing what seemed to be real snow boots and a hat that suggested he had taken winter seriously for the first time in his life.

"Good morning," he said, slightly out of breath. "I may have over-prepared for this."

"You bought snow pants," Dawn observed.

The sporting goods store told me they are essential for maximum mobility in snow-related construction work.

"You went to a sporting goods store."

"I went to three sporting goods stores. Apparently, there are different types of snow pants for different types of snow activities." Thomas looked down at himself with mild bewilderment. "I may have been oversold."

Dawn found herself smiling despite her best efforts to maintain appropriate partner professionalism. "You look like you're about to climb Mount Everest."

"I was going for 'prepared' and landed on 'ridiculous,' didn't I?"

"A little. But I would say 'committed ridiculous'. That counts for something."

Amy cleared her throat with the subtle authority of someone who had schedules to keep. "The contest starts in ten minutes. You should probably strategize."

"Strategize snowman building?" Dawn asked.

"This is Holly Falls. People plan everything carefully." Amy noted on her clipboard. "I'll be judging, so don't expect favoritism just because you're my sister."

"What about favoritism because I'm charming and delightful?" Thomas asked.

"You might try that approach, but it hasn't worked for Dawn in thirty years."

Amy walked away to gather the other contestants, leaving Dawn and Thomas standing in the snow with ten minutes to plan whatever they were about to try.

"So," Thomas said. "Snowman building. I should probably mention I've never actually built a snowman before."

Dawn stared at him, eyes wide with astonishment. "Never? Not even as a kid?"

"We didn't get much snow where I grew up. And when we did, I wasn't exactly…" He paused, editing himself mid-sentence the way he always did when personal details got too specific. "There wasn't really an opportunity."

The air horn sounded before Dawn could ask the follow-up questions that were forming in her throat. Around the square, teams sprang into action amidst the organized chaos of people who took snowman building very seriously.

"Okay," Dawn said, surveying their assigned space. "Basic snowman. Three sections, getting smaller. We start with the base."

"How big should the base be?"

Dawn looked around at the other teams, who were already rolling snow with the efficiency of people who'd clearly done this before. "Big enough to support everything else. Small enough that we don't run out of snow. Medium big."

"Medium big," Thomas repeated. "Very technical."

"I'm making this up as I go along. Work with me here."

They started rolling snow. Thomas approached the task with the methodical precision Dawn was beginning to recognize as his default mode, carefully packing the snow, checking its roundness, and testing its stability at regular intervals.

Dawn, meanwhile, was operating on pure instinct and increasingly creative problem-solving.

"The proportions are wrong," she announced after they'd been working for fifteen minutes.

"You said it was perfect two minutes ago."

"I was wrong two minutes ago. Keep up." Dawn started reshaping their middle section, which had somehow become more oval than round. "We need something distinctive. Everyone's doing traditional snowmen. We need an edge on the competition."

"Edge in snowman form?"

"Exactly." Dawn paused in her snow-restructuring to observe the competition. Mrs. Patterson and her partner were creating what looked like a snowman family with snow-children. The Henderson twins had prioritized height over creativity; their snowman was nearly seven feet tall and still growing.

That's when Dawn spotted the abandoned beach bucket near the edge of their workspace.

"Beach snowman," she said suddenly.

"I'm sorry?"

"Beach snowman. He's on vacation, escaping the cold." Dawn headed toward the bucket, her creative mind shifting into the mode that makes her good at photography but terrible at practical planning. "Irony, Thomas. Comedic irony."

"Irony in snowman form."

"You're catching on."

For the next thirty minutes, Dawn guided their snowman building with the focused intensity she usually reserved for perfect shots. Thomas proved surprisingly helpful during execution; his careful precision worked well for shaping the structural elements, while Dawn handled creative vision and what she generously called "artistic direction."

Their snowman turned out to be anything but traditional. They used a beach bucket as a hat. Thomas built a surprisingly realistic surfboard from a piece of cardboard left nearby. Dawn made sunglasses from dark leaves and designed a Hawaiian shirt pattern using more leaves and some red berries she found under a nearby bush.

"He looks like he's about to catch a wave," Thomas said, stepping back to assess their work.

"That's the point. He's totally out of place, just like everyone feels sometimes." Dawn adjusted the sunglasses, which were slightly crooked. "He doesn't fit, but he's making it work anyway."

Thomas looked at her with an expression she couldn't quite read. "I like that."

The judging process was swift and carried out with the kind of serious deliberation typically reserved for Supreme Court decisions. Amy and the other judges moved from snowman to snowman, taking notes and discussing what seemed to be technical criteria Dawn couldn't even begin to guess at.

When they announced the results, Mrs. Patterson's snowman family took first place. Second place went to Dawn and Thomas's surfing snowman, which the judges declared "unexpectedly charming and creative within the bounds of acceptable snowman parameters."

"We were robbed," Dawn said as they received their second-place ribbon.

"We built a surfing snowman in Indiana in December," Thomas pointed out. "We're lucky we weren't disqualified for geographical impossibility."

The contest merged into the larger Winter Carnival, featuring hot chocolate stands, carousel rides that had been adapted for winter, and enough string lights to be visible from space. As evening fell, the carnival shifted from a daytime family event to a more romantic scene, with couples strolling between booths and the sound of laughter drifting across the snow.

Dawn found herself walking with Thomas through the cooling evening, her second-place ribbon tucked into her coat pocket like a small victory.

"Thank you," Thomas said as they passed the hot chocolate stand.

"For what?"

"For teaching me how to build a snowman. For not making me feel ridiculous when I admitted I'd never done it before." He paused. "For making it fun."

There was something in his voice that made Dawn look at him more closely. "It was just a snowman contest."

"It was the first thing I've ever made that I was proud of."

The words hit Dawn differently than she expected. Not the snowman part, but the first thing I've ever made part. Like someone who grew up supervising rather than doing, managing rather than creating.

"You've never made anything you were proud of?" she asked gently.

Thomas was quiet for a moment. "I've managed things. Overseen things. Made decisions about things other people made." He gestured back toward their snowman, which was still visible across the square, slightly ridiculous and perfectly confident. "But actually making something with my hands? Something that existed because I made it exist? That's... rare. For me."

Dawn felt the weight of his words, sensing the careful distance between himself and hands-on creation. Another piece of the puzzle that was Thomas Miller, who could discuss event management like an expert but treated pinecone-wiring as if it were advanced mathematics.

They had wandered to the far edge of the square, near the old gazebo that was the focal point of most of Holly Falls' outdoor celebrations. It was strung with white lights and decorated with garland, and Dawn realized too late that it was also adorned with mistletoe. Lots of mistletoe. The Holly Falls Parks Department went all out on mistletoe every year.

Thomas noticed it at the same moment she did.

"That's a lot of—"

"Mistletoe. Yeah." Dawn stopped walking. They were now under the gazebo's edge, and there was a particularly large sprig directly above them, impossible to ignore once they'd both spotted it.

"We could walk around," Thomas said.

"We could."

Neither of them moved.

Dawn had been under mistletoe before. She knew the protocol: laugh it off, peck on the cheek, make a joke about holiday traditions and move on. It didn't have to mean anything.

But Thomas was looking at her as if it meant something. Like he wanted it to mean something. And she was standing here with snow in her hair and the memory of their hands working together on something silly and perfect, and she thought:

What am I so afraid of?

The answer was immediate: *This. Exactly this.*

"Dawn," Thomas said, his voice quiet. "I'm not going to kiss you just because there's mistletoe."

"No?"

"No. If I kiss you, I want it to be because you want me to. Not because of a plant."

Her heart was doing something impossible in her chest. "That's very... principled of you."

"I have occasional principles."

"Occasional."

"I'm not perfect."

She laughed, and it came out shakier than she intended. "What if I want you to?"

Thomas went very still. "Then I'd say you should be sure. Because I don't think I can kiss you just once. And you don't seem like someone who does things halfway."

It was a challenge. It was also a warning. He was giving her an escape, a way to step back, blame the mistletoe, act like this moment wasn't happening.

Dawn thought about her wish, tucked inside Nana's ornament. *A place to land. Someone who won't make me stay.*

Thomas wasn't forcing her to do anything. He stood perfectly still, letting her decide.

"I'm not sure," she said. "I'm never sure. But I'm—" She took a breath. "I'm tired of running from things that scare me."

She stepped forward. Rose on her toes. Kissed him.

It wasn't a perfect kiss. Her nose bumped his. She was off-angle at first. But then his hands came up to steady her, one on her waist, one cradling the back of her head, and the angle shifted, and it was—

Oh.

Oh.

He kissed her as if he'd been thinking about it and waiting for the moment. His mouth was warm, tasting of the hot chocolate they shared earlier. The kiss deepened, and Dawn's mind stopped forming words entirely.

When they separated, both of them were breathing heavily. The snow continued to fall. The lights kept twinkling. Nothing was different, yet everything had changed.

"Wow," Thomas said.

"Yeah."

"That was—"

"Yeah."

They were still close, his hand resting on her waist. She knew she should step back, tell a joke, or do something to lighten the moment before it felt too real.

"I'm going to blame the mistletoe," she said.

"That's fair."

"Even though it wasn't the mistletoe."

"I know." He looked at her with an expression she couldn't quite understand, tender, scared, and hopeful all at once. "I know it wasn't."

They walked back toward her parents' house in comfortable silence, Thomas's hand occasionally brushing hers until the third time, when she let him take it. The second-place ribbon was still in her pocket, and their surfing snowman was still visible across the square, and Dawn had the strange sensation of crossing a line she couldn't uncross.

At her door, Thomas stopped, still holding her hand.

"I should—" He gestured vaguely at the night.

"Yeah."

"But I'll see you tomorrow?"

"Tomorrow," she nodded. "Gala stuff."

"Gala stuff." He was smiling, that uncertain smile she was starting to recognize. "Dawn..."

"Don't." She didn't know what she was stopping him from saying, but she knew she wasn't ready to hear it. "Not yet. Let me just—I need to—"

"Okay." He didn't push. "Okay."

He squeezed her hand. Let go. Walked away.

Dawn went inside. The house was quiet, her parents in bed, and Amy was presumably at Will's. She stood in the dark hallway, her back against the door, and pressed her fingers to her lips.

She'd kissed him.

She'd *wanted* to kiss him.

And now there was no taking it back, no pretending it was just holiday spirit, proximity, or convenience. She'd made a choice. She'd stepped toward something instead of away from it.

The panic overwhelmed her in waves. Dawn sat on the bottom step, resting her head in her hands.

What had she done?

Harold the Reindeer stared at her from the living room, his wild eyes offering no comfort and no judgment, just the steady gaze of someone who'd seen this coming from the beginning.

"Don't look at me like that," she told him.

Harold continued staring.

Dawn sat on the stairs until the panic eased into something more manageable, not fear exactly, but the understanding that tomorrow would be different. That she would have to face Thomas knowing they'd crossed a line, and that whatever happened next was going to matter in ways she wasn't ready for.

For now, though, she was home. Safe. The taste of hot chocolate lingered, along with the memory of warm hands and the strange, terrifying realization that she might have just found something worth staying for.

Even if the thought scared her more than anything else possibly could.

Chapter 9:
Awkward Aftermath

D awn woke up early and couldn't fall back asleep.

Not by choice.

Every time she closed her eyes, she felt the kiss again, Thomas's hands steadying her, the way he'd said wow like he meant it, and the snow falling around them like the world's most clichéd blessing. She finally gave up on sleep and did what she always did when feelings became too big: she moved.

By 6 AM, she was at the Busy Bean, nursing coffee she didn't want and pretending to read a newspaper she wasn't really processing. By 7 AM, she'd texted Thomas:

Running errands. Meet at the town hall at 10 for the planning session?

His response came quickly: *Sure. Everything okay?*

Dawn looked at the message for a full minute. She typed and deleted three different responses before finally settling on: *Fine. Just busy. See you at 10.*

She wasn't fine. She was the complete opposite of fine. But "fine" was a wall she knew how to build, and she'd become very skilled at construction over the years.

The next three hours were a whirlwind of productive panic. Dawn picked up the fabric samples they'd ordered for centerpieces. She confirmed vendor contracts. She stopped by the community center to check on the gala venue and discovered the heating system was making a noise that sounded suspiciously like a death rattle.

She called the maintenance guy, who couldn't come until tomorrow. She called Amy to vent about heating systems and vendor requirements and the seventeen different ways their gala could turn into a disaster. Amy didn't answer, probably with Will, feeling happy and settled and all the other things Dawn seemed unable to be.

By 9:45, Dawn had achieved more in four hours than she normally did in two days. She was also worn out, a little manic from too much caffeine, and still hadn't come to terms with the fact that she'd kissed Thomas Miller under a gazebo like some kind of romantic comedy heroine.

She walked to the town hall with five minutes to spare and found Thomas already there.

He'd set up at the large table in the meeting room, papers spread out, laptop open, two coffee cups waiting. Of course, he'd brought her coffee. Of course, he was prepared, organized, and thoughtful because Thomas Miller was seemingly incapable of being anything less than perfect, which made what had happened between them about seven thousand times more complicated.

"Hey," he said when she walked in.

"Hey."

They looked at each other across the table, and the kiss was right there, hanging in the air between them, impossible to ignore. Thomas's mouth opened as if he was about to say something, probably about last night, something honest and vulnerable that would require Dawn to respond in kind.

Dawn cut him off with a flood of gala logistics.

"So the heating system is making concerning noises, which means we might need backup warmth solutions. The fabric samples arrived, but the burgundy appears more purple than I expected. I confirmed the vendor contracts, but Harriet wants to know if we need her to provide serving utensils or if we're handling that separately."

Thomas blinked. "Good morning to you, too."

"Good morning. Sorry. I'm just… there's a lot to do." Dawn sat down and opened her folder with the focused intensity of someone who was definitely not avoiding emotional conversations. "We should probably review the timeline again. Make sure we're not missing anything critical."

"Okay." Thomas's voice was carefully neutral. "Let's review the timeline."

They dove into planning, and it was easier with tasks divided between them. Safer. The burgundy-that-was-actually-purple became a fifteen-minute discussion about color theory and lighting. The vendor coordination turned into a complex flowchart of responsibilities and backup plans.

Dawn observed Thomas carefully as they worked, trying to find clues about his true nature beneath his polite, friendly exterior. He had surprisingly detailed opinions on traffic flow and sight lines that seemed oddly specific.

"You've done this before," she said, watching him sketch out an optimal layout for the registration table.

"Event planning? Not exactly."

"But you know about crowd management and space utilization."

Thomas paused his sketching. "I've been to many events. Corporate functions, charity galas. You start noticing what works and what doesn't." He met her eyes. "When you're responsible for making sure everything runs smoothly, you pay attention to details."

There it was again, the careful editing. The truth that seemed to be missing crucial pieces. Dawn opened her mouth to ask what kind of responsibility he was talking about, but before she could speak, the meeting room door burst open.

Edna Morrison appeared first, dusted with flour and visibly upset, followed by Marv Peterson looking like someone drafted into a chore he didn't choose.

"There you are," Edna said, pointing at Thomas with the authority of someone who'd run out of patience. "You. Come with me. We need a tiebreaker."

Thomas looked bewildered. "A tiebreaker for what?"

"The bake sale display case. My pecan pie versus his chess pie." Edna gestured at Marv with the kind of disdain usually reserved for war criminals. "We can't agree on placement, and the committee is useless."

"I didn't volunteer for this," Marv said mildly. "I was just trying to drop off my pie."

"Your pie is fine," Edna said through gritted teeth. "It's your attitude that's the problem."

Dawn watched this unfold with the fascination of someone witnessing small-town politics in action. "Maybe you could both—"

"No," Edna said firmly. "We tried compromise. Compromise doesn't work when one person is being completely unreasonable about display hierarchy."

Thomas looked at Dawn helplessly. "I don't know anything about... uh... pie politics."

"That's what makes you neutral," Edna said, already grabbing his arm. "Come on. This won't take long."

"I can keep working," Dawn said quickly. "On the vendor coordination. I'll just... keep working here."

Thomas hesitated. "You sure?"

"Absolutely. Take your time."

The truth was, Dawn needed a minute without him. Needed space to breathe and think and figure out why her chest felt tight every time he looked at her with that patient, understanding expression.

After they left, Dawn tried to concentrate on vendor lists and timeline coordination. She read the same line four times before realizing that the words weren't sinking in. The issue wasn't the gala. The issue wasn't heating systems, purple burgundy, or pie display politics.

The problem was that she'd kissed Thomas Miller and truly meant it, enjoyed it, and didn't know how to handle that.

Her phone buzzed with a text from Thomas: *Chess pie won. Marv is insufferable about it. Edna is plotting revenge. I fear for next year's bake sale.*

Despite herself, Dawn smiled. She typed back: *You survived pie politics. That's basically a rite of passage in Holly Falls.*

What doesn't kill you makes you stronger?

What doesn't kill you makes you qualified for the town council.

Noted. I'll update my resume.

The easy banter felt natural, familiar. Like they could return to being co-chairs, friends, and jokesters about small-town drama without the complications from last night.

Except Dawn still felt his hands on her waist. She could still taste the hot chocolate and the unique sweetness of choosing something that scared her.

Thomas returned twenty minutes later, smelling like pie crust and looking a bit shell-shocked.

"How bad was it?" Dawn asked.

"Edna has very strong opinions about proper pie presentation. Also, Marv might be the most passive-aggressive person I've ever met, and I've worked in corporate America."

"Welcome to Holly Falls. Everyone is very passionate about their specific areas of expertise."

Thomas sat down across from her, and suddenly the relaxed atmosphere shifted. He was looking at her with that careful attention she was starting to recognize, as if he was trying to read something she wasn't ready to reveal.

"Dawn," he said quietly. "Can I say something? About last night?"

Dawn's stomach clenched. "Thomas—"

"I don't regret it. Whatever happens next, I don't regret kissing you."

The words hit her like a physical blow. She clenched her pen tighter, staring down at the vendor contracts she couldn't understand.

"I'm not good at this," she finally said. "Staying true to my word. Following through. I have a pattern."

"What if I'm willing to take that risk?"

"Then you're braver than me."

Thomas was quiet for a moment. "Maybe. Or maybe I just think you're worth it."

The words hit deep, in places Dawn had guarded carefully for years. She felt something break inside her chest, something warm and frightening rushing up to the surface.

"We should finish the vendor list," she said, deflecting with the skill of someone who'd mastered the art of emotional avoidance. "And figure out the backup heating situation. Focus on the gala."

Thomas's expression flickered with hurt but quickly concealed behind understanding. "Sure. The gala. That makes sense."

They worked for another hour with careful politeness, discussing logistics, timelines, and practical details that felt manageable. Safe. When they finally gathered their papers and headed for the door, Thomas walked her home like he always did, but something had shifted between them.

At her door, he didn't linger like he had the night before. He offered a polite smile that wasn't his genuine one and said goodnight.

"Thomas," Dawn said as he turned to leave.

He stopped. Waited.

She wanted to say something. She wanted to take back the deflection, the careful distance she'd put between them. She wanted to be brave enough to acknowledge what was happening instead of running from it.

"Thanks for the coffee," she said instead. "And for handling the pie crisis."

"Anytime."

He walked away, and Dawn went inside feeling like she'd just pushed away the first real thing she'd had in years.

Amy came down the stairs while Dawn was standing in the dark hallway, still wearing her coat.

"Dawn? What happened?"

"Nothing," Dawn said as she headed for the kitchen. "I need wine."

"It's Tuesday afternoon."

"Your point?"

Amy followed her, watching Dawn pour a glass and drain half of it before speaking again.

"Did something happen with Thomas?"

Dawn stared at the kitchen wall. "I told him we should focus on the gala."

"And?"

"And he said okay."

Amy waited for more explanation. When none came, she poured her own glass. "That sounds... reasonable?"

"It was." Dawn finished the wine. "That's the problem."

"I'm not following."

Dawn set down her empty glass and looked at her sister. "He said he didn't regret kissing me. Said I was worth the risk. Said all the right things." She paused. "And I told him we should focus on work and figure things out later."

"Ah." Amy's expression shifted to understanding. "Classic Dawn Donovan emotional avoidance maneuver."

"I'm not avoiding anything. I'm being practical."

"You're being scared."

"Same thing."

Amy was quiet for a moment. "What are you afraid of?"

Dawn thought about the question. About Thomas's hands steadying her under the mistletoe. About the way he'd looked at their ridiculous surfing snowman like it was the most important thing he'd ever created. About how easily he'd fit into her family's living room, wearing her father's sweatshirt as if he belonged there.

"That it's real," she finally said. "That it matters. That I could actually want to stay somewhere long enough to see what happens next."

"And that terrifies you."

"That terrifies me."

Amy nodded as if that made perfect sense. "So you're sabotaging it before it can hurt you."

"I'm being careful."

"You're being scared," Amy repeated. "And that's okay. But Dawn?" She met her sister's eyes. "You can't run from everything good just because it might end badly. Sometimes the risk is worth taking."

Dawn reflected on Thomas's expression when she had deflected his vulnerability—the pain he tried to hide and the polite smile that wasn't genuine.

"I think I already messed it up," she said.

"Then fix it."

"What if I can't?"

Then at least you'll know you tried instead of wondering what might have happened if you had been brave enough to find out.

That night, Dawn lay in bed gazing at the glowing stars and contemplating courage, risk, and the cruelness of wanting something you are afraid to pursue. Harold the Reindeer watched from the dresser, his unblinking eyes offering no judgment or answers.

Tomorrow she'd have to see Thomas again. She would have to pretend everything was normal while knowing she'd chosen safety over possibility, fear over hope.

But tonight, she simply lay in the dark and wondered if Amy was right. If some risks were worth taking, even when they felt like leaping off a cliff with no guarantee of landing safely.

Even when landing safely, Dawn Donovan had never been particularly good at it.

Chapter 10:
Sister's Day Out

Amy showed up at Dawn's bedroom door early the next morning with a box of supplies and a serious look on her face.

"Get up. We're baking."

Dawn pulled the pillow over her head. "No."

"It's for the charity drive. We committed. Get up."

"You committed. I was hijacked."

"Same thing." Amy yanked the pillow away with the ruthless efficiency of someone who's been dealing with Dawn's avoidance tactics for thirty years. "Also, you've been weird for two days, and I'm staging an intervention disguised as holiday cheer."

Dawn squinted at her sister through sleep-messed hair. "That's manipulative."

"I learned from the best. Mom sends her love. Now get up."

Dawn got up, partly because Amy clearly wasn't leaving, and partly because she'd been lying in bed replaying the same conversation with Thomas for hours, which was driving her slightly insane.

Twenty minutes later, she was in the kitchen, staring at what looked like Amy's attempt to recreate the entire baking aisle of a grocery store.

"Why four types of cookies?" Dawn asked, observing the chaos of ingredients Amy somehow put together while she was getting dressed.

"Because Mrs. Patterson requested variety and donated three hundred dollars to the community center, so Mrs. Patterson gets variety."

"You're very precise for someone who claims to love Christmas."

"Hush. Start creaming that butter."

They worked in companionable quiet for the first hour. Amy was precise, measuring carefully, following recipes to the letter, keeping a mental list of what was in the oven. Dawn was... less methodical. She estimated measurements. She tasted the cookie dough more than she should. She got distracted by how the morning light hit the flour dust in the air.

"That's too much vanilla," Amy observed, watching Dawn dump what was definitely more than a teaspoon into the mixer.

"There's no such thing as too much vanilla."

"There objectively is. There's a recipe."

"Recipes are suggestions."

"Recipes are instructions."

"Agree to disagree."

They had this argument before. They would have it again. It felt familiar and comforting, like how sisters argue over small things because the big issues are too difficult to express directly.

The first batch of sugar cookies went into the oven. Dawn was rolling out dough for the second batch when Amy said, too casually:

"So, are you going to tell me what's going on with Thomas, or are we just going to pretend you've been avoiding the house for two days because you suddenly love errands?"

Dawn's rolling pin stuttered across the dough. "I haven't been avoiding—"

"You went to the hardware store three times, but we don't need anything from the hardware store."

"I was comparing... paint samples."

"You hate paint samples. You told me once that paint samples are 'capitalism's way of making you feel bad about your walls.'"

Dawn didn't have a response to that, mainly because Amy was absolutely right and they both knew it.

Amy set down her measuring cup and turned to face her sister fully. "Dawn. Talk to me."

"There's nothing to talk about."

"You kissed him."

Dawn's head snapped up. "How do you—"

"Edna told Mom. Mom told me. Holly Falls, remember? Nothing is secret."

"Edna wasn't even there."

"Edna knows everything. It's her superpower." Amy leaned against the counter. "So. You kissed him. And now you're spiraling."

"I'm not spiraling. I'm... processing."

"You're avoiding. There's a difference."

Dawn wanted to argue, but she couldn't, mainly because Amy was right about that, too.

The tension in the kitchen grew as they kept working. Dawn kept rolling the dough, pressing too hard and leaving the rolling pin stuck where the dough had gotten too thin. Amy kept watching with that knowing look that made Dawn want to scream.

"Stop looking at me like that," Dawn said finally.

"Like what?"

"Like you're waiting for me to have a breakdown."

"I'm not waiting. I'm just... present. In case."

"Well, stop being present. Be somewhere else."

"It's my kitchen."

"It's Mom's kitchen."

"Semantics."

Dawn slapped the dough down harder than necessary. Flour poofed into a white cloud, dusting her shirt, the counter, and somehow Amy's hair. She looked at the mess. Looked at Amy.

"This is your fault," Dawn said.

"The flour?"

"All of it. You dragged me to that town meeting. You invited him to the tree farm. You—"

"I didn't make you kiss him."

"No. But you—" Dawn grabbed a handful of flour from the bag. She didn't know what she was going to do with it until she did it.

She threw it at Amy.

It hit Amy square in the chest, a white explosion across her dark sweater that left her looking like a very belligerent snowman had attacked her.

Amy stared down at herself. Looked up at Dawn.

"Did you just—"

"Maybe."

"You're thirty years old."

"And?"

Amy took the bag of flour.

What followed could only be described as warfare. Amy had always been methodical, but apparently that extended to flour fights; she had a strategy, targeting Dawn's hair and somehow managing to get flour down the back of her shirt. Dawn fought back with chaotic enthusiasm, grabbing handfuls and throwing them wildly until the kitchen looked like a winter wonderland had exploded.

Five minutes later, they were both sitting on the flour-dusted floor, backs against the cabinets, laughing that helpless kind of laughter that made your stomach ache.

"Mom is going to kill us," Amy managed between gasps.

"Worth it."

"So worth it."

The timer went off, the first batch of cookies was done, but neither of them moved to get up.

"I'm scared," Dawn said.

She didn't intend to say it. It just slipped out in the quiet after the chaos, like the flour fight had loosened something.

Amy turned to look at her, flour in her eyelashes. "Of Thomas?"

Dawn picked at a clump of flour on her jeans. "Of how much I like him." I kissed him, Amy. I chose to kiss him. I didn't get swept up or surprised. I looked at him, and I wanted to, so I did.

"That sounds... healthy?"

"It's terrifying." Dawn's voice cracked. "Because now I can't pretend it's not real. I can't tell myself it's just proximity or holiday spirit or whatever. I like him. A lot. And I don't know what to do with that."

Amy was quiet for a moment, considering. When she spoke, her voice was careful.

"Do you remember when I came home last year? Before Will?"

"You mean when you were a control-freak mess who made color-coded schedules for Christmas dinner?"

"Yes. That." Amy almost smiled. "I was so sure I had everything figured out. The plan, the timeline, the perfectly organized life. And then Will happened, and suddenly everything I thought I wanted just... didn't matter anymore."

"That's different. You wanted to stay. You wanted the small-town life. I don't—" Dawn stopped. "I don't know what I want."

"I think you do. I think that's what scares you."

Dawn looked at her sister, really looked. Amy, covered in flour and sitting on the kitchen floor, was being more honest than either of them usually managed.

"What if I let him matter," Dawn said slowly, "and then I have to stay? Really stay, not just visit. And what if I stay and I lose myself? What if I become someone who makes color-coded schedules and measures vanilla precisely and never goes anywhere new?"

"Is that what you think happened to me?"

"I believe you found something worth staying for. I believe you found someone who turned the idea of roots into growth rather than a trap."

Amy was silent for a long moment. "You know what I was most afraid of with Will?"

"That he'd see through your organizational superpowers and realize you're actually a mess like the rest of us?"

"That I'd convince myself it was too risky. That I'd talk myself out of it before I gave it a real chance." Amy's voice was soft. "I spent so much time being afraid of losing him that I almost lost him by not letting him in."

"And now?"

"And now I wake up every morning grateful that I was brave enough to let him see the real me. Even the messy parts. Especially the messy parts."

Dawn considered this. "What if the real me is someone who runs when things get complicated?"

"Then maybe the real Thomas is someone who's willing to run with you. Or wait for you to come back, or convince you that some things are worth staying for." Amy reached over and brushed flour out of Dawn's hair. "You've been running so long you've forgotten why you started. Running isn't freedom, Dawn. It's just movement. It's also a way of life that you have become accustomed to."

The words hit harder than Dawn expected. She sat there, covered in flour in her mother's kitchen, and realized she couldn't remember the last time she'd stayed somewhere because she wanted to, rather than because she had to.

***

Forty miles away, Thomas Miller was sitting in the Holly Falls Inn's small sitting room, staring at his phone and trying to decide whether to send the text he'd typed and deleted several times.

Eric found him there at mid-afternoon, silver-haired and immaculately dressed as always, carrying the kind of authority that came from forty years of legal practice and an unfortunate tendency to be right about everything.

"Thomas." Eric settled into the chair across from him with the satisfaction of someone who'd driven from Indianapolis specifically to deliver unwelcome advice. "How's the undercover philanthropy going?"

"Eric, I wasn't expecting you."

"Your assistant mentioned you'd gone dark. No one's seen hide nor hair of you for two weeks. The board is starting to ask questions." Eric studied Thomas with the sharp attention that had made him one of the most respected lawyers in the state. "Have you told her who you are?"

Thomas set down his phone. "I've told her some things."

"That's splitting hairs, and you know it."

"It's complicated."

"It's simple. You're lying to someone you care about. The only complicated part is how you're going to fix it."

Thomas stood up and moved to the window overlooking Holly Falls' main street. From there, he could see the town square, the gazebo where he'd kissed Dawn three nights ago, and the Christmas tree that somehow looked both magical and ridiculous in the afternoon light.

"My father was never appreciated for who he truly was," Thomas said quietly. "Everything was about what he had. What he could provide. What he could do to benefit others' bottom lines."

"Your father was a complicated man."

"He was lonely. He spent forty years being wanted for his money and died wondering if anyone would have loved him without it."

Eric was silent for a moment. "And you think you're avoiding that by hiding what you have?"

"I believe I'm trying to figure out who I am when money isn't involved."

"Noble. Also impossible," Eric's voice was gentle but firm. "Money isn't the only thing about you, Thomas. But it is part of you. The philanthropy, the foundation, the choices you make about how to use what you have, that's character. Hiding it isn't protecting anyone. It's just another form of dishonesty."

Thomas turned away from the window. "What if she runs when she finds out?"

"Then she runs. But at least she'll be running from the real you, not from a version of yourself you made to be more acceptable."

"And if she stays?"

"Then she stays because she chose you. All of you. The man who can't wire a pinecone and the man who runs a foundation that has donated forty million dollars to education initiatives. Both of those people are you, Thomas. You don't get to pick and choose which parts matter."

Thomas pulled out his phone again, looked at the draft text he d been writing and deleting: *Can we talk? There's something I need to tell you.*

"The gala is in five days," he said.

"So?"

"If she reacts badly or needs space to process, it could ruin everything. The event matters to her and the community."

"And?"

"And maybe it's better to wait until after, when the timing isn't so—"

"Thomas." Eric's voice interrupted his attempt at rationalization. "You're not protecting her. You're protecting yourself. There will never be a perfect time for tough conversations.

Thomas looked at the message. His thumb hovered just above the send button.

He thought about Dawn covered in snow, rising on her toes to kiss him. About the way she had taught him to wire pinecones, patient and encouraging. About how she looked when she laughed, unguarded and bright.

He thought about the anonymous donation he'd made to save the bake sale, about the careful way he answered questions about his background, and about the growing burden of maintaining a story that was true but incomplete.

Thomas deleted the text.

He typed a new one: *Hope you're having a good day. Let me know if you need anything for the gala.*

Professional. Friendly. Safe.

He sent it and immediately hated himself for being a coward.

***

Back in the Donovan kitchen, Dawn's phone buzzed with a message from Thomas.

"What does it say?" Amy asked, watching Dawn read.

"He's being polite."

"Is that bad?"

"It's—" Dawn put the phone down. "It's what I asked for."

She'd wanted space. He was giving it to her.

So why did it seem like they were further apart than ever?

"I should apologize," Dawn said. "For pushing him away."

"Probably."

"But I don't know what to say. 'Sorry I panicked' doesn't seem like enough."

"Sometimes it's exactly enough." Amy stood up, brushing flour off her jeans. "You don't have to have it all figured out, Dawn. You just have to show up."

Dawn looked around the disaster zone they had created. Flour was everywhere, cookies were half-baked, and her sister was covered in evidence of their food fight. It was chaos. It was messy. It was exactly the kind of beautiful disaster that happens when you stop trying to control everything and just let things unfold.

Maybe Amy was right. Maybe just showing up was enough.

But first, they had to clean the kitchen before their mother came home and found out what happened when Dawn Donovan tried to ignore her feelings by baking, and her sister called her out on it.

Some disasters, after all, demand immediate attention.

Chapter 11:
Thin Ice

Three days of polite texts had been three days too many. Dawn was wrapping centerpiece candles at the community center when Amy found her, moving with the focused determination of someone on a mission.

"You're going to the Winter Carnival tonight," Amy announced.

"I'm busy," Dawn replied, not looking up from the candle she was systematically destroying with ribbon.

"You're wrapping candles. That's not busy, that's hiding."

"It's productive hiding."

Amy took the mangled candle from Dawn's hands before she could cause more damage. "Thomas is running the raffle booth tonight. For the gala. You're partners, remember? You should probably check on him."

"I can check on him through text."

"Dawn."

"What?"

Amy sighed, the kind of sigh that carried an entire conversation about sisterly frustration and loving frustration.

Three days ago, you told me you wanted to apologize. It's been three days. Either talk to him or admit you're letting this go.

Dawn didn't answer right away. She picked up another candle and began wrapping it more carefully than any candle in the history of centerpieces ever had.

Amy set down her supplies. "Carnival starts at six. The raffle booth is near the gazebo. I'm not going to make you go, but I think you should."

After Amy left, Dawn stared at the half-wrapped candle in her hands. Three days of being a coward were enough. She knew this. She just didn't know what she was going to say when she saw Thomas's face.

I'm sorry seemed insufficient. *I panicked* felt incomplete. *I'm terrified of how much I like you* was probably more honesty than either of them was ready for.

But Amy was right about one thing: texting wasn't going to solve this.

The Winter Carnival in Holly Falls was its most lively and festive. Booths lined the town square like a temporary village, with string lights hanging between lampposts and trees, creating a golden canopy overhead. The makeshift ice rink had been set up where the fountain usually sat, and the air was filled with the scents of mulled cider, kettle corn, pine, and woodsmoke.

Dawn walked through the crowd, telling herself she was just here to check on gala preparations. Nothing more complicated than that.

She spotted Thomas before he spotted her.

He was behind the raffle booth, talking to a family with three small children about ticket packages and prize options. He was wearing Doug's too-small sweatshirt—he still hadn't returned it, apparently—and he was smiling, but Dawn recognized it as his professional smile. The one that was warm and engaging but didn't quite reach his eyes.

He looked exhausted. He looked just like she felt.

Dawn nearly turned back around, almost convinced herself that a carefully worded text would be enough to bridge the gap she'd created between them.

But then Thomas looked up and saw her.

Something shifted in his expression, surprise, wariness, and beneath it all, hope. The professional smile faded into something more uncertain, more genuine.

"Hi," Dawn said when she reached the booth.

"Hi." Thomas finished with the family, handed over their raffle tickets, and turned his full attention to her. "How are the centerpieces coming?"

"I've only destroyed two of them so far. Amy intervened before I could do serious damage."

"That's progress."

They looked at each other across the booth, and Dawn felt the weight of three days of careful politeness, of conversations that only touched on logistics, schedules, and safe topics.

"Can I say something?" Dawn asked.

Thomas nodded.

"I'm sorry for what I said the other day, for pushing you away. I got scared, and when I do, I push people away—it's my default. She gripped the edge of the booth. "But you don't have to apologize for what you said. You were honest, and I wasn't ready for honesty."

"Dawn—"

"I do because I didn't mean it. Not the part about waiting, not the part about focusing on work instead of—" She gestured vaguely between them. "I meant the part about being scared. That was true. But the rest of it was just my fear talking."

133

Thomas was quiet for a moment. "What are you scared of?"

Dawn looked around the carnival, watching families walk between booths, couples drinking hot chocolate, and children running past their parents with the unconscious confidence of people who knew they belonged somewhere.

"That I'll want to stay," she finally said. "That I'll want to stay so badly that I'll lose myself trying to become someone who's good at staying."

"What if you don't have to become someone else? What if you could just... be yourself somewhere?"

"I'm not sure if I know how to do that."

Thomas came around the booth to stand beside her. "We could figure it out together."

"Is that what you want? To figure it out?"

"Yes." No hesitation. "If you're willing to let me try."

Dawn felt something loosen in her chest, something that had been tight and guarded for three days. "I think I'd like that."

A customer approached the booth, and they resumed working together as if the last three days never happened, with Thomas explaining the prizes while Dawn handled the ticket sales, finding their rhythm again as if they'd never lost it. It was mundane work, repetitive and simple, but Dawn found herself relaxing into it.

"I need you to know something," she said during a lull between customers.

"What?"

"Running was the scarier option. Staying and trying to figure this out with you, that's actually the brave choice for me."

Thomas looked at her with an expression she couldn't quite read. "Thank you for telling me that."

"Thanks for making it seem like a choice rather than a trap."

After an hour of booth duty, Thomas convinced someone from the volunteer committee to take over, and they wandered through the carnival together. Dawn noticed details she had missed on her way in, how the lights reflected off the snow, the sound of children's laughter blending with holiday music, and the smell of cinnamon from the pastry booth.

"Want to try ice skating?" Thomas asked as they passed the makeshift rink.

Dawn looked at him skeptically. "Have you ever ice skated before?"

"How hard can it be?"

"Famous last words."

Thomas was, as it turned out, spectacularly bad at ice skating.

He made it approximately three feet from the edge before his ankles wobbled and he grabbed for the railing with the desperate grip of someone who'd just realized they'd made a terrible mistake.

"Okay," he said, not moving from his death grip on the rail. "This is harder than it looks."

"You're terrible at this," Dawn observed, gliding over to him with the easy confidence of someone who'd grown up in Indiana winters.

"I said it was hard. I didn't say I was good."

"Here." Dawn took his hands, gently prying them away from the railing. "The key is not fighting it. You have to trust the skates to do what they're designed to do."

"What if I fall?"

"Then you fall. I'll help you get back up."

For the next twenty minutes, Dawn led Thomas around the rink at a pace that could generously be called cautious. He was thorough about it, asking questions about weight distribution and balance, treating it like a problem to be solved rather than a skill to be felt.

"You don't make me feel stupid for not knowing this," Thomas said as he successfully completed a turn without grabbing for support.

"Why would I? Everyone's bad at things until they learn how to do them."

"Not everyone is patient with the learning process."

Dawn studied his profile as they glided slowly along the edge of the rink. "What kind of things were you supposed to learn instead of ice skating?"

Thomas was silent for a moment. "Running a company. Managing people. Being responsible for things that mattered."

"How old were you when you started learning those things?"

"Twelve, maybe? Formally. But really, I think I've been preparing for it my whole life." He glanced at her. "There was always someone else to do the fun stuff. I was supposed to be learning the important stuff."

"Ice skating isn't important?"

"Ice skating is..." Thomas stopped moving, standing still in the middle of the rink. "Ice skating is for people who have time for things that don't produce measurable outcomes."

Dawn felt a twinge of sympathy for the twelve-year-old Thomas, who was learning responsibility instead of having fun. "And now?"

"Now I think maybe I've been measuring the wrong outcomes."

They skated until Thomas's ankles gave out and Dawn's cheeks were pink from the cold, then found themselves at the bonfire that had been set up near the gazebo. Someone had arranged hay bales in a circle around the fire, and couples and families sat sharing blankets and hot chocolate.

Thomas returned from the cider stand with two steaming cups, and they found a spot on one of the bales, sitting close enough that Dawn could feel the warmth radiating from his shoulder.

"Can I ask you something?" Thomas said after they'd sat in comfortable quiet for a few minutes.

"Sure."

"What would you do if you could do anything? No practical considerations, no financial constraints, no need to be sensible. What would you build if you could build anything?"

Dawn was caught off guard by the question. "That's a dangerous question to ask someone who's spent their whole life avoiding long-term commitments."

"I'm willing to risk it."

Dawn looked into the fire, watching sparks rise and vanish into the dark sky. "There's this barn on the edge of town. The Peterson place. It's been empty for years, red walls, sagging roof, completely impractical." She paused. "I keep thinking it would make an amazing studio. Not just for me, but for anyone who wanted to create things. A pottery wheel, easels for painting, space for photography, room for workshops. An arts collective, I guess."

"That sounds amazing."

"It sounds impractical. I don't know anything about running a collective, or business licenses, or how to maintain a building that's probably structurally unsound."

"You could learn," Thomas said. "And you could find people who know the things you don't know."

"You make it sound possible."

"Maybe it is possible."

Dawn turned to study his face in the firelight. "What about you? What would you build?"

Thomas was quiet for so long that Dawn thought he wasn't going to answer. When he spoke, his voice was careful.

"I have more money than I know what to do with," he said finally. "A lot more. The kind of money that changes how people see you, how they interact with you. When people know what I have, they see the money first."

Dawn's stomach tightened slightly. "How much more?"

"Enough that it gets complicated," Thomas stared into the fire. "I've been responsible for this company since my father died three years ago. Important decisions, thousands of employees, and more money than most people see in a lifetime. And I'm good at it; I can manage budgets, negotiate deals, and make the kind of choices that matter on spreadsheets."

He turned to look at her. "But I've never built a snowman. I've never ice skated. I've never sat around a bonfire with someone I—" He stopped, seeming to edit himself. "With someone who likes me for reasons that have nothing to do with what I can provide."

"What would you build?" Dawn asked again, gently.

"Something real," Thomas said. "Something that matters because it makes people happy, not because it's profitable. I want to know what it feels like to create something with my hands that exists just because I wanted it to exist."

Dawn felt something shift in her chest, something warm and terrifying and impossibly hopeful.

They sat by the fire until the carnival started winding down, until families began gathering their children and couples started walking home through the snow. When they finally got up to leave, Thomas grabbed her hand.

"Dawn," he said. "I need you to know this isn't a game for me. I'm not just passing through Holly Falls for the novelty of it."

"You said you're leaving after Christmas."

"I said I was here through Christmas. That's not the same thing."

Dawn looked at their intertwined hands, at Thomas's serious face in the fading firelight, and at the snow starting to fall around them like the world's most perfect timing.

"I'm done running from things that scare me," she said. "Which means I need you to stop running too."

She stepped forward and kissed him.

This kiss was different from the one under the mistletoe. This wasn't tentative or uncertain or prompted by holiday tradition. This was Dawn's choice, made in full awareness and with clear intention. This was her stepping toward something instead of away from it.

Thomas's arms came around her, and he kissed her back like he'd been waiting for this moment for weeks. Like he'd been hoping she'd choose him the way he'd already chosen her.

When they broke apart, both breathing hard, Dawn felt steadier than she had in years.

"This doesn't mean everything's fixed," she said.

"I know."

"We have a lot to figure out."

"I know that too."

"But this is a start."

"This is definitely a start."

They walked home hand in hand through the falling snow, and Dawn found herself thinking about the Peterson barn, about arts collectives and impossible dreams, about the way Thomas had said *something real* like it was the most important thing he'd ever wanted.

At her door, they stopped.

"Tomorrow?" Thomas asked.

"Tomorrow."

"There are things I need to tell you," he said. "Things I need to figure out how to say."

Dawn was so focused on the way he was looking at her and on the memory of his arms around her that she didn't question what he meant. Whatever it was, it could wait. This—them, together, choosing each other—was enough for now.

"Okay," she said. "When you're ready."

Thomas squeezed her hand and walked away, while Dawn went inside feeling like she'd just made the most important decision of her life.

She lay in bed that night replaying every moment of the evening, the apology, the ice skating disaster, the conversation by the fire, the kiss that felt like coming home to something she'd never known she was looking for.

Things I need to tell you. Things I need to figure out how to say.

The words followed her into sleep, a small question mark in the corner of her happiness. But Dawn pushed it away. Whatever Thomas needed to tell her, whatever he was struggling to figure out, it couldn't be that important.

Could it?

Chapter 12:
Disaster in the Kitchen

The following week, Dawn was reviewing final gala preparations at the community center when Mayor Posey arrived, her expression that of someone delivering catastrophic news.

"We have a problem," the mayor said without preamble.

Dawn looked up from her clipboard, which had become disturbingly similar to Amy's organizational systems. "What kind of problem?"

"The ten-thousand-dollar kind."

Dawn's stomach dropped. "What do you mean?"

"Franklin Motors." Mayor Posey sat down heavily at the table. "They just pulled out. Something about 'restructuring priorities' and 'challenging economic conditions.' Corporate speak for 'we're not giving you money this year.'"

Dawn stared at the budget spreadsheet in front of her. Franklin Motors wasn't just a sponsor; they were the anchor sponsor. Their ten thousand dollars covered venue rental, catering deposit, and decorations, leaving enough buffer for unexpected expenses.

"The gala is in four days," Dawn said.

"I'm aware of the timeline."

"We can't just—that money pays for everything. Without it, we don't have a gala. We have a very expensive party that no one can afford to host."

"I've already called every business in town," Mayor Posey said. "No one can cover that kind of gap on this timeline. Most of our local sponsors are already tapped out for the year."

Dawn stared at the numbers that no longer added up. Without Franklin Motors, they were twelve thousand dollars short of breaking even. Even with aggressive cost-cutting, they'd still be eight thousand dollars in the red.

"What do we do?"

"I was hoping you'd have an idea."

Dawn called Thomas because she needed to tell someone, and he was the person she wanted to tell. Not because she expected him to fix it—what could he do?—but because saying it out loud to him would help her think.

"Ten thousand dollars," she said when he answered. "Four days' notice."

Thomas listened while she explained the situation. She could hear him thinking on the other end of the line, that particular quiet that meant his brain was working through possibilities.

"How much do you need?" he asked finally.

"Ten thousand minimum. Ideally, twelve, to have a buffer for emergencies."

"And you have four days."

"Three and a half, really. The venue needs final payment by Friday morning, or they will release our date to someone else."

Silence. Then: "What if we held an emergency fundraiser? Something fast, high-visibility."

"Like what?"

"I don't know yet. But we have the whole town. Everyone wants the gala to succeed. What if we gave them a way to help?"

It wasn't a quick solution, but it was a direction, which was more than Dawn had five minutes ago.

"Can you meet me at Harriet's Bakery in an hour?" Dawn asked. "I have an idea, maybe."

***

After he hung up, Thomas sat in his room at the Holly Falls Inn, staring at his phone.

Ten thousand dollars. He could solve this in five minutes. One phone call to Marcus, his assistant. An anonymous donation from one of his foundation's discretionary funds. The foundation donated more than that every month to various causes; this would barely register as a line item.

He picked up the phone. Put it down.

If he did this, if he fixed it with money, he'd be using exactly what he'd been hiding from Dawn. Even if no one knew, he would know. It would be one more lie between them, one more way he was manipulating their relationship with resources she didn't think he had.

But if he didn't, and the gala failed, and Dawn lost something she'd poured herself into...

Thomas picked up the phone again.

Dialed.

"Marcus, I need you to do something, and I need you to be discreet about it."

***

The emergency bake sale plan came together with the kind of desperate efficiency that only happens when there is no time to do things properly.

The concept was simple: transform Harriet's Bakery into fundraising central tomorrow afternoon. Every donation welcome, with all proceeds going to the gala fund. They'd promote it through the church phone tree, the school email list, and the Holly Falls Facebook group, which somehow reached every resident within six hours of any posted news.

"It won't raise ten thousand dollars," Amy said when Dawn explained the plan.

"I know. But it'll raise something. And it shows the town we're trying instead of just giving up."

"What about the rest?"

"I don't know yet. One crisis at a time."

The next eighteen hours were a blur of logistics and frantic coordination. Dawn handled vendor relationships and venue negotiations. Thomas managed communications and volunteer scheduling. Amy bullied every family she knew into donating baked goods. Patricia Donovan called in decades of social favors with the efficiency of a general mobilizing a small army.

By the next morning, Harriet's Bakery was overflowing with cookies, pies, cakes, breads, and mysterious confections that Dawn couldn't identify but that smelled incredible.

"This is either going to be amazing or a complete disaster," Dawn said, surveying the chaos.

"Those aren't mutually exclusive," Thomas pointed out, testing the stability of a table that was sagging under the weight of seventeen different varieties of Christmas cookies.

"You've mentioned that before."

"It keeps being true."

The sale officially started at noon. By 12:15, they'd already hit their first crisis.

Thomas, who'd been assigned to the pie table after promising that "selling pie can't be that complicated," managed to sell Edna Morrison's competition pie to Mrs. Henderson. The problem: that pecan pie was Edna's entry in next week's pie competition. Not for sale. Definitely not for sale.

"You sold my competition pie?" Edna's voice could have cut through steel.

"It had a price tag," Thomas said defensively, holding up a small piece of masking tape.

"That said 'EDNA MORRISON, PECAN.' It was my entry identification, not a price tag."

"I thought that was... the flavor description?"

Dawn had to intervene before Edna committed justifiable homicide. She smooth-talked Edna into a replacement entry slot, tracked down Mrs. Henderson, and negotiated the pie's return. The negotiations were complicated because Mrs. Henderson had already eaten a slice and declared it "quite good, though the crust could use work."

By 1 PM, the sugar cookie table had literally collapsed. The folding legs gave out under the weight of thirteen dozen elaborately decorated cookies, sending them cascading onto the floor in a shower of frosting and broken dreams.

By 2 PM, Dawn had frosting in her hair, flour on her face, and a burn on her wrist from grabbing a hot pan without thinking. Thomas had given incorrect change to at least four people and had been gently but firmly banned from the cash box.

"I'm not good at this," he admitted, watching Dawn efficiently bag Mrs. Patterson's brownie order while simultaneously answering questions about cookie ingredients and directing traffic.

"You're terrible at this," Dawn agreed.

"I said not good. Terrible seems harsh."

"You told Mr. Patterson his wife's brownies were 'interesting.'"

"They were interesting!"

"Interesting is not a compliment when it comes to baked goods, Thomas. It means you're not sure whether they're food or a science experiment gone wrong."

But here was the surprising thing: the chaos was working. People weren't just buying things and leaving; they were staying, chatting, and pitching in when disasters struck. Mrs. Patterson's "interesting" brownies sold out first because everyone wanted to see what Thomas had found so fascinating.

The Henderson twins appointed themselves the official table repair crew after the cookie collapse. Turns out, they only lost two dozen to breakage. Despite the pie incident, Edna stayed to help with crowd control. Even Mayor Posey rolled up her sleeves and started bagging purchases when the line grew too long.

By 4 PM, when they finally tallied the day's receipts, they'd raised four thousand dollars.

Four thousand. Not nearly enough to save the gala, but four thousand more than they'd had that morning. It felt like hope, even if it wasn't quite salvation.

They were in the cleanup phase, Dawn wiping down tables while Thomas swept up frosting crumbs, when Mayor Posey burst back through the door with an expression Dawn couldn't read.

"You're not going to believe this," the mayor said.

"What now?" Dawn asked, prepared for another crisis.

"I just got a call from First Federal Bank. Someone made an anonymous donation to the gala fund. It was deposited directly this afternoon."

Dawn's heart jumped. "How much?"

"Eight thousand dollars."

The bakery fell silent. Dawn dropped her cleaning cloth. Thomas stopped sweeping mid-stroke.

"Eight thousand?" Dawn repeated.

"Eight thousand." Mayor Posey was grinning now. "The bank can't tell me who, but the donor requested full anonymity. Someone just saved the Christmas Gala."

Dawn did the math automatically: four thousand from the bake sale plus eight thousand from an anonymous donation equaled twelve thousand total. They weren't just saved; they had the buffer they'd hoped for.

"Who would donate eight thousand dollars anonymously?" Dawn asked.

"I have no idea. Maybe someone from out of town? Someone with connections to the community?"

Dawn turned to Thomas, wanting to share her relief, disbelief, and overwhelming gratitude.

His expression stopped her cold.

Thomas wasn't surprised. He wasn't celebrating. He looked... guilty. Like someone who'd been caught doing something they shouldn't have done.

"That's amazing," he said, but his voice was all wrong. Too controlled, too careful.

"Are you okay?" Dawn asked.

"Fine. Just—tired. Long day."

Dawn was too relieved and too busy processing the magnitude of their salvation to push. She hugged Mayor Posey, called Amy to share the news, and started mentally rearranging their budget to take advantage of the unexpected windfall.

She didn't notice Thomas step outside. She didn't see him lean against the building, eyes closed, breathing like someone who'd just done something he couldn't take back.

After everyone else had gone home, Dawn and Thomas were the last ones left, sitting on the curb outside the bakery as the sun set over Main Street.

"We did it," Dawn said, still not quite believing it.

"You did it. I mostly made things worse."

"You sold a competition pie to a woman who ate it before we could get it back. That's a very specific kind of chaos."

"I contain multitudes."

Dawn laughed, the kind of exhausted laughter that came from surviving a crisis you weren't sure you'd survive. "Thank you. For being here today. For all of it."

"I didn't do much."

"You did enough." She leaned against him, and it felt natural now, the physical closeness and the assumption that his shoulder was a place she belonged. "I couldn't have handled today without you."

Thomas was quiet. His arm came around her, but there was tension in him, something coiled tight within him.

"Dawn."

"Mm?"

"There's something I need to tell you."

Her contentment wavered. She lifted her head to look at him, and the seriousness in his voice made her stomach clench.

"That sounds ominous."

"It's important." He wasn't looking at her. He was staring at the darkening street, the Christmas lights just beginning to flicker on in shop windows. "I've been wanting to tell you for a while. I just—I didn't know how to."

"Thomas. Whatever it is—"

"It's about who I am and what I haven't told you." He swallowed hard. "The anonymous donation—"

Dawn's whole body went still. "What about it?"

For a moment, she thought he was going to say it. Whatever he'd been carrying, whatever had been making him look guilty rather than relieved. His mouth opened, and she could see him gathering his courage.

Then his phone buzzed. He glanced at it reflexively, and the moment shattered.

"Sorry. I need to take this. Work thing."

"You have a work thing?"

"Client. Freelance." He was already standing, already creating distance. "I'll call you later, okay? We can talk then."

"Thomas—"

"I promise. Tonight. We'll finish this conversation."

He walked away before she could respond, phone pressed to his ear, leaving Dawn sitting on the step with a growing knot of unease in her stomach.

The anonymous donation.

She replayed Mayor Posey's words. *Someone from out of town. Someone with connections to the community.*

Thomas had appeared in Holly Falls two weeks ago. Eight thousand dollars was a lot of money for most people, but Thomas had said he had "more money than he knew what to do with." He'd been evasive about his work, his background, and his family's business.

And when Mayor Posey announced the donation, Thomas looked guilty rather than surprised.

Dawn sat on the step as the street grew dark around her, adding up the clues she'd been ignoring.

At home, she found Amy in the kitchen, making tea and looking as if she'd been waiting for her.

"How did it go?" Amy asked.

"We raised four thousand dollars, and then someone made an anonymous donation of eight thousand more."

"That's incredible! Who?"

"That's the eight-thousand-dollar question." Dawn sat down at the kitchen table. "Amy, can I ask you something?"

"Sure."

"If someone was lying to you, not about everything, just about one big thing, would you want to know?"

Amy's face sharpened with immediate attention. "What are you talking about?"

"Hypothetically."

"That's not a hypothetical question, Dawn. That's a 'my sister suspects something' question." Amy sat down across from her. "What's going on?"

Dawn stared at her hands, trying to organize thoughts that felt too big and too scary to say aloud.

"I think Thomas might not be who he says he is."

The words hung in the air between them, and Dawn realized she'd been thinking it for days without letting herself. All the little inconsistencies, the careful answers, the way he approached manual tasks as if he'd never had to do them before.

"What makes you think that?"

"Eight thousand dollars, Amy. Who has eight thousand dollars just lying around? Who can afford to donate that much money anonymously to a small-town Christmas gala?"

"Maybe someone who cares about you?"

"Or maybe someone who has a lot more money than he's been letting on."

Dawn thought about Thomas's expression when the donation was announced. About the expensive rental car and the careful way he talked about his background. About how he'd said he had "more money than he knew what to do with" but made it sound modest rather than significant.

"What are you going to do?" Amy asked.

"I don't know. He was trying to tell me something about the donation tonight. But then his phone rang, and he left and—" Dawn shook her head. "I should just ask him directly."

"Should you?"

"Shouldn't I?"

Amy was quiet for a moment. "Dawn, if he's been lying about something big, there's probably a reason. And finding out what that reason is... that might change everything."

Dawn knew Amy was right. But sitting in her mother's kitchen, thinking about Thomas's guilty expression, his mysterious work calls, and the way he'd looked when he'd started to tell her something important, she realized she wasn't sure she was ready for everything to change.

Not when she'd just figured out she wanted it to stay exactly the way it was.

Chapter 13:
Secret on the Brink

Dawn woke thinking about the anonymous donation. She'd gone to bed telling herself it didn't matter who'd given eight thousand dollars to save the gala. The money was there, the crisis was resolved, and speculating about mysterious benefactors was pointless.

But she kept thinking about Thomas's expression when Mayor Posey announced the donation. Not surprised. Not celebratory. Guilty.

She pushed the thought away and went downstairs to find Candace Oren sitting at the kitchen table with her mother, drinking coffee and wearing the expression of someone who'd been waiting to share interesting news.

"Good morning, sweetie," Patricia said. "Candace stopped by to check on the final gala preparations."

"Actually," Candace said with a smile that was just sharp enough to catch Dawn's attention, "I wanted to ask about Thomas. I hope he's feeling better."

Dawn poured herself a cup of coffee, keeping her face neutral. "Feeling better?"

"Oh, he seemed so tired this morning. I saw him in the inn's hallway around six, on what sounded like a very important business call." Candace's eyes were bright with curiosity. "Very official-sounding. Something about legal documents and acquisitions."

Dawn's coffee mug paused halfway to her mouth. "He was on a business call at six AM?"

"Oh yes. Very intense conversation. He mentioned something about Miller Enterprises. That's quite a company, isn't it? I looked it up after I heard him say the name. Fascinating what you can find online these days."

The words hit Dawn like ice water. Miller Enterprises. Thomas Miller. How had she not made that connection?

"Well," Dawn said carefully, "Thomas does consulting work. I'm sure he has clients in different time zones."

"Oh, I'm sure he does," Candace agreed, though her smile suggested she'd found something far more interesting than consulting work.

After Candace left, Dawn sat in the kitchen, staring at her untouched coffee. Miller Enterprises. She could look it up herself. She should look it up. But if she did, she might find out things she wasn't ready to know.

Instead, she grabbed her coat and headed for the community center, telling herself she had work to do.

She made it three blocks before changing direction toward the library.

The Holly Falls Public Library had four ancient computers in the back corner, all of them slower than dial-up internet and twice as frustrating. Dawn sat down at the least broken one and typed: "Miller Enterprises."

The results loaded slowly, line by line, like a revelation she couldn't stop.

Miller Enterprises. Headquarters in New York. Founded 1987. Current CEO: Thomas Miller.

Dawn clicked on the leadership page.

The professional headshot that loaded was unmistakably Thomas. Same eyes, same face, wearing a suit that probably cost more than Dawn earned in three months. The caption read: Thomas Miller, Chief Executive

Officer. Mr. Miller assumed leadership of Miller Enterprises following his father's death in 2022. Under his guidance, the company has expanded its philanthropic initiatives while maintaining its commitment to sustainable growth.

Net worth: estimated at 2.3 billion dollars.

Dawn stared at the screen until the words stopped making sense.

She clicked through article after article. Business profiles describe Thomas as a "low-profile but effective leader." News stories about company acquisitions, charitable donations, and board meetings. Photos of him at charity galas and corporate events, always in expensive suits, always looking exactly like someone who ran a billion-dollar company.

Everything he'd told her was true. His father had died three years ago. He worked for a company. He was involved in philanthropic initiatives.

It had also been an enormous lie.

By the time Dawn left the library, she had forty-seven minutes to get home and pretend everything was normal for the family dinner she'd invited Thomas to before she knew he was one of America's richest men.

Thomas arrived at exactly seven o'clock, carrying flowers for her mother and looking like the same person who'd taught her to wire pinecones and couldn't figure out how to use a staple gun. He was wearing Doug's sweatshirt, the 1987 Indiana State sweatshirt belonging to a man who taught high school and drove a fifteen-year-old sedan.

Dawn watched Thomas charm her family and answer their questions with the same careful honesty he'd always used, and felt as if she were observing a stranger.

"What do your parents do, Thomas?" Patricia asked over dessert.

"My father was in business," Thomas said easily. "He passed away a few years ago."

All technically true, but missing the part about him being the CEO of a multi-billion-dollar corporation.

"I'm sorry for your loss," Doug said. "That must be especially difficult during the holidays."

"It is. But this—" Thomas gestured around the table, "—this makes it easier. Being part of a family, even temporarily, does."

Even temporarily. Dawn's chest tightened.

"You're not temporary," Amy said warmly. "You're stuck with us now."

Thomas smiled, but Dawn caught a flicker of something across his face. Guilt? Sadness? She couldn't tell anymore.

After dinner, Amy cornered Dawn in the kitchen while Thomas helped Doug with something in the garage.

"What's wrong?" Amy asked. "You've been weird all evening."

Dawn set the plates she was clearing down with more force than necessary. "Do you remember what Candace said this morning about Thomas's phone call?"

"The business thing? I assumed she was being dramatic. You know how catty she can be."

"She wasn't being dramatic." Dawn lowered her voice. "I looked it up. Miller Enterprises. It's huge, Amy. Billions of dollars. And Thomas—" She stopped, swallowed hard. "He's not just an employee. He's the CEO."

Amy's face went through several expressions: confusion, disbelief, understanding.

"Holy shit."

"Yeah."

"The guy who can't use a staple gun is a billionaire?"

"Apparently."

156

Amy leaned against the counter. "Have you talked to him about it?"

"No. I just found out earlier today at the library. I've been sitting through dinner, pretending everything's normal while my brain melts."

"You need to talk to him."

"I know."

"Tonight. Before you spiral completely."

"I'm not spiraling."

"Dawn, you're absolutely spiraling." Amy squeezed her arm. "Look, I don't know why he didn't tell you. Maybe there's a good reason. But you need to hear it from him."

Dawn nodded, her hands shaking slightly. "I'll walk him out after dessert. We'll talk."

"Good." Amy hesitated. "For what it's worth, the way he looks at you isn't fake. Whatever else is going on, that part's real."

Dawn wanted to believe that. She wasn't sure she could.

After dessert, Dawn walked Thomas out into the cold December night. The Christmas lights reflected off the snow, and everything looked exactly like a perfect small-town Christmas postcard.

They reached the end of the walkway before Dawn stopped.

"We need to talk."

Thomas turned, and something in his expression shifted. Recognition. Resignation. As if he'd been waiting for this moment and dreading it equally.

"Dawn—"

"Miller Enterprises." She said it flatly, without inflection. "You're Thomas Miller. The CEO. Billionaire Thomas Miller."

He didn't deny it. He didn't try to deflect or explain. He just stood there in the falling snow, looking as if she'd just delivered a physical blow.

"Yes."

One word. No excuses. No elaborate explanations.

"How long were you going to let me believe you were a freelance consultant?"

"I was going to tell you. I've been trying to tell you—"

"When? After Christmas? After the gala? After I fell completely in love with you?"

The words were out before she could stop them, hanging in the cold air between them like an accusation and a confession, rolled into one.

Thomas's entire face changed.

"You're in love with me?"

Dawn felt exposed, raw. "Don't. Don't make this about that."

"You said—"

"I said a lot of things. Most of them before I found out you've been lying to me for two weeks."

"I didn't lie about who I am," Thomas said quietly. "I lied about what I have. Everything between us is real."

"How am I supposed to believe that? I don't even know you. The Thomas I thought I knew doesn't exist."

"Yes, he does." Thomas stepped closer, and Dawn could see the desperation in his eyes. "The man who couldn't wire pinecones, whom you taught to ice skate, who wore your father's sweatshirt and felt like part of your family for the first time in his life, that's me. That's exactly who I am."

"You're worth two billion dollars."

"That's what I have. It's not who I am."

Dawn laughed, but there was no humor in it. "Do you hear yourself? You think money isn't part of identity when you have that much of it?"

"When my father died, I inherited a company I never wanted and responsibilities I never asked for. Every person I meet sees the money first. Every relationship is complicated by what I can provide." Thomas's voice cracked. "You were the first person in three years to see me instead of my bank account."

"Because you lied about it!"

"Because you didn't know about it. And for two weeks, I got to find out who I was when money wasn't part of the equation."

Dawn stared at him, snow collecting in her hair. "The anonymous donation. That was you."

Thomas nodded. "Yes."

"Eight thousand dollars. Just... poof."

"I have it. It was there. The gala needed it. What was I supposed to do?"

"Tell me! You were supposed to tell me before you made a decision that affected something I was responsible for."

"Would you have accepted it if you'd known it came from me?"

Dawn opened her mouth to say yes, then stopped. Because he was right. If she'd known Thomas Miller, CEO, was offering to solve their financial problems, she never would have accepted it.

"That's not the point."

"Isn't it?"

They stood there in the falling snow, and Dawn felt that everything she'd thought she knew was shifting beneath her feet.

"I need time," she said finally. "To process this. To figure out what's real and what's not."

Thomas nodded. "Okay."

"Don't text me tonight. Don't try to explain or fix this. Let me sit with it for now."

"I understand."

"Do you?" Dawn's voice was softer than she intended. "Because I just found out that the man I fell in love with is someone I've never actually met."

Thomas looked as if she'd slapped him. "Dawn—"

"Goodnight, Thomas."

She turned and walked back to the house without looking back. She knew he was standing in the snow for a long moment before she heard his footsteps heading toward the street.

Inside, Dawn closed the door and leaned against it, breathing hard. Her chest felt tight, as if she couldn't get enough air.

Amy found her sitting on the stairs, head in her hands.

"He's worth two billion dollars," Dawn said without looking up.

"I know."

"Two billion, Amy, with a B. I was worried about him spending eight thousand dollars on the gala donation."

Amy sat down beside her. "What did he say?" she asked.

"That everything between us was real. That he lied about what he had, not who he was." Dawn's voice cracked. "How am I supposed to tell the difference?"

"Did he feel real? When you were together, did it feel like he was pretending?"

Dawn thought about Thomas, tangled in Christmas lights, looking at her family's tree as if he'd never seen one decorated with love. About him giving Harold the Reindeer a name without hesitation. About the way he'd said the first thing I've ever made that I was proud of after their ridiculous snowman.

"No," she whispered. "It felt like the most real thing I've ever had."

"Then maybe that's your answer."

"Or maybe I'm just really bad at recognizing when someone's lying to me." Dawn looked at her sister. "I told him I loved him. It just came out, and now I don't know if any of it was true."

Amy put an arm around her. "You don't have to know tonight. Tonight, you just feel it. Tomorrow, you figure out what to do."

Dawn leaned against her sister and finally let herself cry. For the man she'd thought she knew. For the relationship that felt both more real and more impossible than anything she'd ever experienced. For the terrifying possibility that love and deception might not be mutually exclusive.

Somewhere in the snow, Thomas was walking back to the inn, carrying the weight of his secret, finally spoken aloud. Tomorrow, they'd both have to decide what to do with the truth.

Tonight, they were just two people who'd found each other at Christmas and then lost each other just as quickly.

Chapter 14:
The Discovery

D awn hadn't slept. Early the next morning, she was still staring at the ceiling, replaying Thomas's expression when she'd confronted him. The simple "Yes" that held no excuses, no elaborate explanations. The way his whole face had changed when she'd accidentally confessed her love for him.

Her phone showed three messages from Thomas, sent between midnight and 2 AM:

I'm sorry.

I know that doesn't fix anything, but I need you to know.

Whenever you're ready to talk, I'll be here.

She stared at the messages until they blurred. Then she turned her phone face down and tried to pretend sleep was possible.

Two hours later, Amy knocked on her door and came in.

"Coffee's ready downstairs," Amy said, settling on the edge of Dawn's bed without invitation. "How are you holding up?"

"I'm fine."

"That's a lie."

"That's a lie," Dawn agreed.

Amy was quiet for a moment. "Can I ask you something?"

Dawn nodded.

"Did you fall in love with a lie, or with the guy who couldn't use a staple gun, wore Dad's ugly sweatshirt, and looked at you like you hung the moon?"

"I don't know the difference anymore."

"I think you do." Amy's voice was gentle. "Everything you told me about him, the way he fits with our family, the way he listens when you talk, the way he looks at Harold as if that reindeer were actually offering wisdom, none of that changes because he has money."

"Everything changes because he has money, Amy. The power dynamic, the reason he's here, whether any of it was real or just some kind of—" Dawn stopped. "Rich guy slumming it in small-town America."

"Is that what you think?"

Dawn didn't answer, mostly because she didn't know.

By 10 AM, the news had spread through Holly Falls with the efficiency of small-town gossip networks. Dawn discovered this when she walked into the Busy Bean for coffee and three conversations stopped mid-sentence. She didn't know how everyone found out, but she knew the town knew. Probably Candace.

She ordered a large coffee and a muffin she didn't want, paid with exact change, and left without making eye contact with anyone. But she caught fragments:

"—two billion dollars—"

"—Candace said she heard him on the phone—"

"—makes you wonder what he really wants—"

At the community center, Mayor Posey was waiting for her.

"Dawn, I think we need to talk."

The conversation was excruciating. Mayor Posey had legitimate questions about the anonymous donation, Thomas's involvement with the gala, and whether Dawn had known who he was. Dawn answered as honestly as she could, which meant admitting she'd found out last night and was still processing.

But it wasn't just the mayor. Word had spread with supernatural speed, and everyone wanted to talk about Holly Falls' unexpected billionaire visitor.

Mrs. Patterson cornered her by the punch bowls, wanting to know whether the romance was "real or some kind of publicity stunt." Edna demanded to know whether the pie incident had been deliberate sabotage by "big city interests." Even sweet old Mr. Hendricks wanted to know whether Thomas might be interested in funding a community arts initiative.

Dawn smiled. Deflected. Felt herself crumbling inside.

This was supposed to be hers. The gala. The holiday. The tentative hope that maybe she'd found something worth staying for. Now it was all tangled up in Thomas's money, her humiliation, and the entire town watching to see what would happen next.

She escaped to the back hallway, leaned against the wall, and tried to catch her breath.

That's where Thomas found her.

He looked as bad as she felt, exhausted and pale, still wearing her father's sweatshirt, which now seemed almost absurd, given that she knew he could probably buy her parents' entire neighborhood without checking his bank balance.

"I heard," he said. "About Candace. The town knowing."

"Everyone knows. It's literally the only thing anyone's talking about."

"I'm sorry. I know this makes everything harder."

Dawn looked at him, really looked. "Are you? Sorry?"

"That you're dealing with fallout from my choices? Yes. That the secret's out?" He paused. "I don't know. Maybe it's better this way."

"Better how?"

"No more lies between us, not even by omission."

Dawn felt something twist in her chest. "You think that fixes this? The town knowing?"

"No, but I think it's a start." Thomas moved closer, and she could see the careful hope in his eyes. "Dawn, what happened last night—"

"I can't do this here." She gestured toward the hallway, where muffled sounds of gala preparation echoed beyond. "Not with half the town watching."

"Then where?"

"I don't know. I don't know anything right now." Dawn rubbed her temples. "Thomas, I need to ask you something, and I need you to be completely honest about it."

"Okay."

"Why are you really here in Holly Falls? The real reason."

Thomas was quiet for a long moment. "I was tired. That's the truth. Three years of running a company I inherited, making decisions I never wanted to make, and being responsible for things I didn't understand. I came here because I wanted to disappear for a while."

"And I was what? A convenient distraction?"

"You were—" He stopped. Then started again. "You were the first person in years to see me as just a person. Not as Thomas Miller, CEO. Not as a dollar amount. Just... Thomas."

"Because I didn't know who you were."

166

"Because you saw who I was beneath all the rest of it." His voice was quiet. "Dawn, everything I told you about myself was true. My father died three years ago. I work for a company. I was lonely. I did want something real."

"You just left out the part about being worth more than most countries' GDPs."

"Yes."

Again, that simple honesty that somehow made everything worse.

They stood there in the hallway, and Dawn felt the weight of the entire town's curiosity pressing against the walls.

"I need to get back," she said finally. "People are expecting updates."

"Dawn—"

"Tomorrow, we get through the gala. Together. As co-chairs." She met his eyes. "After that, I don't know. But we committed to this thing, and I'm not going to let the community down because my personal life is a mess."

"I understand."

"Do you?"

"I understand that you're protecting yourself and that you have every right to."

Dawn felt something crack in her chest. "I'm not—"

"Yes, you are. And that's okay. I should have told you sooner I should have trusted you with the truth instead of hiding behind omissions and carefully prepared answers." Thomas's voice was steady. "I made this mess. I don't expect you to clean it up."

"But you want me to."

"I want you to forgive me. I want you to believe that what we had was real. I want you to give us another chance." He paused. "But I understand if you can't."

Dawn stared at him. At this man who'd somehow become essential to her sense of what Christmas felt like, who'd integrated himself into her family so seamlessly that she'd started taking his presence for granted. Who'd lied to her for two weeks about something fundamental.

"The gala," she said. "We finish the gala. Then we talk. Really talk."

"Okay."

"Don't make any grand gestures. Don't try to fix this with money or expensive gifts or whatever billionaires do when they want something."

"I won't."

"And Thomas?" She turned to go, then looked back. "For what it's worth, I believe you when you say your feelings were real. It's just that I don't know if that's enough."

That evening, Amy found Dawn at the kitchen table, staring at her phone.

"Are you going to call him?"

"I already texted him. We're working together tomorrow night, and then we'll see."

Amy sat down across from her. "Can I tell you something?" she asked.

"Sure."

"If Thomas had told you on day one that he was a billionaire CEO, would you have given him a chance?"

Dawn opened her mouth to say yes, then stopped. "Probably not."

"Why?"

"Because..." Dawn thought about it. "Because I would have assumed he was slumming it, looking for a quaint small-town experience to tell stories about at cocktail parties, or that he was the kind of person who had adventures instead of relationships."

"And now?"

"Now I've seen him tangled in Christmas lights. I've watched him wear my dad's ugly sweatshirt as if it were tailored specifically for him. I've seen him look at our Christmas tree as if he'd never seen one decorated with love before." Dawn's voice grew smaller. "And I know that none of that was fake."

"So what are you afraid of?"

Dawn was quiet for a long time. "That it doesn't matter. That good intentions and real feelings aren't enough to bridge the gap between what our lives look like."

"And what if they are?"

Dawn didn't have an answer to that.

That night, she picked up her phone and typed a message to Thomas:

Tomorrow we get through the gala. Whatever happens after, we face together. As co-chairs.

She stared at it. It wasn't forgiveness. It wasn't even kindness, really. It was just... a door left open.

She hit send.

His response came within seconds:

Together. I'll be there.

And Dawn, thank you. For not giving up on me completely.

She didn't respond, but she didn't block him either. It wasn't much. But it was something.

Tomorrow, the gala. Tomorrow, they'd face the town together, or apart. She hadn't decided yet.

But tonight, she fell into a deep sleep. For the first time since she'd found out the truth, she didn't dream of running.

The fact that she dreamed of Thomas instead, of his hands steady on her waist, of the way he'd said wow after their first kiss, and of the careful hope in his eyes when he'd asked if she could forgive him was something she'd think about later.

When she was ready to figure out what forgiveness meant.

When she knew whether love was enough to bridge the gap between two people who'd found each other by accident and then lost each other just as quickly.

When she decided whether the man she'd fallen in love with was real enough to be worth the risk of staying with him.

***

Thomas set his phone on the nightstand and ran his hands through his hair. Tomorrow, they'd co-chair the gala together, presenting a united front as the entire town watched to see whether their relationship would survive the revelation that had rocked Holly Falls' rumor mill for the past twenty-four hours.

Tomorrow we get through the gala. Whatever happens after, we face together. As co-chairs.

Not as lovers. Not as partners. As co-chairs. Professional collaboration with a woman who'd seen him at his most vulnerable and was still deciding whether he was worth the complexity he'd brought into her life.

He thought about calling Eric, but what would he say? *I found the woman I want to marry and I've managed to royally mess it up by lying about everything except how I feel about her?* Eric would probably point

170

out that Thomas had created this situation himself by choosing deception over honesty from the very start.

But how could he have told her? *Hi, I'm Thomas Miller. I'm worth two billion dollars, and I'm hiding in your small town because I don't know who I am without my father's company. Want to help me figure out how to be normal?*

She would have run. He knew it in his bones. Dawn, who fled from spice drawers and lease renewals, would never have given a billionaire CEO a real chance. She would have been kind and polite, and gone within the week.

Instead, he'd gotten three weeks of her seeing him as just Thomas. Three weeks of learning that he was capable of being someone worth knowing when he wasn't performing the role of CEO. Three weeks of falling in love with a woman who made him want to wire pinecones, wear Doug's terrible sweatshirt, and believe that home was something you chose rather than something you inherited.

And now she knew everything, and she was still willing to stand beside him tomorrow night. It wasn't forgiveness, she'd made that clear. But it was something. A door was left ajar when she could have slammed it shut.

Thomas turned off the light and lay back against the pillows, thinking about the way Dawn had looked at him in the community center hallway. Hurt, yes. Angry, definitely. But also... disappointed. As if she'd hoped for better from him, which meant she'd believed he was capable of it.

Maybe that was enough to build on. Maybe tomorrow night, working side by side to make the gala everything they'd planned, he could show her that the man she'd fallen for was real, even if he came with complications she'd never asked for.

She didn't respond. But he wasn't blocked either. It wasn't much.

But it was something.

THE CHRISTMAS WISH

Chapter 15:
The Dark Moment

Dawn stood in front of her bedroom mirror, looking at herself in the blue dress with silver accents she'd bought specifically for tonight.

It had felt like armor when she'd picked it out three weeks ago, something beautiful, confident, and worthy of the gala she was helping to create. She'd imagined Thomas seeing her in it, pictured his expression, and allowed herself to feel excited about the possibility of dancing with him while their community celebrated around them.

Now it just felt like a costume for a performance she wasn't sure she could deliver.

Her phone buzzed. A text from Thomas: *Break a leg tonight. You've created something beautiful.*

Professional. Supportive. Exactly what a co-chair should text another co-chair.

Dawn stared at the message until her vision blurred, then put her phone away and went downstairs.

The Holly Falls Community Center had been transformed. Walking into the main hall, Dawn barely recognized the space where she'd spent countless hours over the past month. White and silver fabric draped from the ceiling like fallen snow. Centerpieces of pine and silver caught the light from dozens of string lights. The silent auction items were displayed along one wall, and tables were arranged to create intimate conversation spaces while leaving room for dancing.

Their vision, made real.

Thomas was already there, adjusting a centerpiece with the focused attention of someone who needed something to do with his hands. He was wearing a dark, perfectly tailored suit, probably worth more than Dawn's monthly rent. He looked every inch the CEO she now knew him to be.

When he saw her, his whole face changed.

"You're here," he said.

"I said I would be."

"I know. I just—" He stopped himself. "You look incredible."

"Thank you." She kept her voice even. Professional. "The room looks good."

"We did good work."

"We did."

They stood there, the decorated room between them, with all the things they weren't saying louder than the Christmas music playing softly from the speakers.

"Dawn—"

"Let's just get through tonight." She cut him off, not unkindly. "We can figure out the rest after."

Thomas nodded. Accepted it. "After."

The doors opened. The first guests arrived, and the gala began.

The night unfolded in a blur of handshakes, small talk, and careful navigation. Dawn worked the room, greeting guests, thanking donors, and accepting compliments on the decorations with a smile that felt increasingly fragile. Everyone was watching her; she could feel it. The sympathetic glances. The curious stares. The whispered conversations that stopped when she approached.

Thomas worked on the other side of the room. They orbited each other without touching, close enough to coordinate when needed and far enough to avoid the questions that would come if they stood together for too long.

It was exhausting. It was also, somehow, working.

The auction went well. The food was praised. The silent auction raised more money than they'd projected. Mayor Posey gave a speech thanking the co-chairs, and Dawn stood next to Thomas as the crowd applauded, feeling as if she were playing a role in someone else's life.

But despite the tension, the whispers, and the careful distance she was maintaining, they were pulling it off. The gala was a success.

During a lull between the main course and dessert, Dawn escaped to a quiet corner near the windows, watching the snow begin to fall more heavily.

Thomas appeared beside her. He didn't say anything at first. He just stood there, both of them watching their reflection in the dark window.

"We did it," Dawn said finally.

"Almost. Another hour."

"The hard part's over."

"Is it?"

She knew he wasn't talking about the gala, so she pretended not to understand.

"The auction hit its target. The venue's paid for. The community center fund is—"

"Dawn." His voice was quiet. "Look at me."

She did. It was a mistake. His eyes were too honest, too vulnerable, too much of everything she'd been trying not to feel.

"I know you don't trust me right now," he said. "I know I haven't earned that back yet. But I need you to know, tonight, watching you work this room, watching you be gracious to people who've been gossiping about you all week—" He shook his head. "You're the strongest person I've ever met. And I'm so sorry I'm the reason you had to be."

Her throat tightened. "Thomas..."

"You don't have to say anything. I just needed you to know."

He turned back to the window. They stood together in silence, watching the snow fall, and for one moment, just one, it felt like before. Like they were just two people who'd found each other at Christmas and discovered something worth protecting.

Then Candace Oren's voice cut through the room.

"—and of course, the question everyone's asking is what happens now?" Candace was holding court near the refreshment table, her voice pitched to carry. "I mean, the gala's lovely, but let's be honest. We all know why he's really here."

Dawn froze. Thomas went still beside her.

"A billionaire doesn't just wander into Holly Falls for the Christmas charm," Candace continued, her laugh sharp and brittle. "There's always an angle. Always a deal. I heard Miller Enterprises is looking at properties in the area. Wouldn't that be convenient? Cozy up to the locals, get the inside track on real estate opportunities—"

"That's not true." Thomas's voice was calm, but Dawn heard the steel underneath.

The room went quiet. Every conversation stopped. Everyone turned to look.

Dawn wanted to disappear. Wanted to run. Wanted to be anywhere but standing next to Thomas while Candace Oren publicly dissected their relationship for the town's entertainment.

But Thomas stepped forward, and when he spoke, his voice carried across the room.

"I didn't come here for business," he said. "I came here because I was tired. Because I wanted one Christmas that wasn't about acquisitions or board meetings or being Thomas Miller, CEO." He paused, and Dawn could see him gathering his courage. "I found something better. I found people who saw me as a person, not a bank account. I found—"

His eyes found Dawn across the room.

"I found someone who made me want to be worthy of being seen."

The silence was absolute.

"My name is on this gala because I wanted to help. The anonymous donation was mine because this community center matters to people I care about. Whatever you think of me, whatever you've heard or assumed, I'm not here to take anything from this town." His voice softened. "I'm here because this is the first place in three years that's felt like home."

He walked toward the door. Not running, walking, with dignity intact. But Dawn could see his hands shaking.

The room erupted in whispers.

Dawn found herself moving. Through the crowd, past the shocked faces and eager gossips, following Thomas without consciously deciding to.

Amy caught her arm. "Dawn—"

"I have to—"

"I know. Go."

She went.

Outside, the cold hit her immediately. She wasn't wearing a coat, hadn't thought to grab one, and the snow was falling harder now, dusting the parking lot and muffling sound.

Thomas stood at the edge of the lot, facing away from the building. His shoulders were rigid with tension.

"Thomas."

He turned. His face was composed, but she could see what it was costing him to hold it together.

"You should go back inside," he said. "It's cold."

"So should you."

"I think I've done enough damage for one night."

"You told the truth. That's not damage."

"Isn't it?" He laughed, but there was no humor in it. "I just announced to the entire town that I'm in love with you, and you can barely stand to be in the same room with me."

"That's not—" Dawn stopped. Started again. "Thomas, what Candace said—"

"What she said doesn't matter. She's right about one thing, though. I am a billionaire who wandered into Holly Falls. I lied about who I was. And now you're dealing with the consequences of my choices."

"Stop." Dawn stepped closer. "Stop making this about protecting me. I'm tired of people making choices for me because they think I can't handle the truth."

"What truth?"

"That I'm terrified." The words came out in a rush. "That I've never felt anything like this before, and it scares me more than anything I've ever experienced. That I spent two weeks falling for someone I thought was completely wrong for me, only to find out he was even more wrong than I imagined."

Thomas flinched.

"But also," Dawn continued, "that everything I fell in love with is still there. The way you look at Harold as if he's offering actual wisdom. The way you fit into my family as if you'd been there all along. The way you said 'wow' after our first kiss, as if it were the most amazing thing that had ever happened to you."

"Dawn—"

"I think I'm in love with you too," she said. "The real you. All of you. The billionaire CEO and the man who can't wire a pinecone. And that terrifies me."

Thomas stared at her. Snow was collecting in his hair, on his suit jacket. "What does that mean?"

"It means I'm done running from the things that scare me." Dawn stepped forward again, close enough to see her breath mingle with his in the cold air. "It means I need you to stop being so perfect when I'm trying to be angry at you."

"I'm not perfect."

"No, you're not. You lied to me for two weeks. Granted, it was by omission. You made decisions about our relationship without consulting me. You have more money than most small countries, which is frankly terrifying from a power-dynamics perspective."

"Dawn—"

"But you also made me believe in Christmas again. You made me want to stay somewhere for the first time in my adult life. You made me feel that home was something I could choose rather than something that would trap me."

Thomas was very still. "What are you saying?"

"I'm saying I choose you. Despite the money. Despite the lies. Despite being absolutely terrified of what loving you might mean." Dawn reached for his hands. "I'm saying I want to figure this out. Together. If you're willing to be honest with me. Really honest. About everything."

"I'll tell you everything. I want to tell you everything."

"Then tell me now. Right here. Whatever I need to know."

Thomas took a shaky breath. "I've been in love with you since you taught me to wire pinecones and didn't make me feel stupid for not knowing how. I've been lying awake every night since we met, trying to figure out how to tell you who I really am without losing you. And when I walk into a room, the first thing I do is look for you, because you make every space feel like somewhere I want to be."

"Thomas—"

"I know it's not enough. I know money changes everything, and I know I should have told you sooner. But everything I said about wanting something real was true. You make me feel real."

Dawn looked at him, snow in his hair, vulnerability written across his face, standing in a parking lot in a suit that probably cost more than her car, looking at her as if she were the only thing in the world that mattered.

She kissed him.

Not like the mistletoe kiss, which had been about Christmas magic and possibility. Not like their second kiss, which had been about choosing connection over fear.

This was about choosing him. All of him. After everything.

His arms came around her, and he kissed her as if he'd been holding his breath for days and could finally breathe again. As if she were everything he'd been hoping for and hadn't dared to believe he could have.

When they broke apart, both breathing hard, Dawn realized she wasn't cold anymore.

"This doesn't mean everything's fixed," she said.

"I know."

"We have a lot to figure out. Logistics. Power dynamics. Whether I can handle dating someone who could buy this entire town without checking his bank account."

"I know that too."

"But this—" She gestured between them. "This is real. This is worth fighting for."

"It's the most real thing I've ever known."

They walked back into the gala together, hand in hand. The whispers followed them, but they were different now, surprised, speculative, maybe even hopeful.

The night continued. People danced. The silent auction concluded with record-breaking results. The gala was officially a success.

Near the end of the evening, the band played a slow song. Dawn and Thomas had been careful all night, working side by side, coordinating without lingering, maintaining just enough distance to keep the gossip to a minimum.

But when Amy caught Dawn's eye and tilted her head toward the dance floor with an expression that clearly said *don't be an idiot*, Dawn made another choice.

"Dance with me?" Thomas asked.

"People will stare."

"Let them."

She took his hand. Let him lead her onto the floor.

They danced. Not perfectly. Thomas was no better at dancing than he'd been at ice skating, but close. His hand warm on her back. Her head fitting against his shoulder as if they'd been designed to fit together.

"So what happens now?" she asked quietly.

"I don't know. I have to deal with my board and figure out the business situation. But I meant what I said. I'm not going anywhere until we figure this out."

"Good. Because I'm done running."

"Yeah?"

"Yeah. I think I might actually want to stay."

The song ended. They stepped apart. Around them, the gala wound down, with people saying goodbyes and volunteers beginning cleanup, marking the successful conclusion of weeks of work and worry.

Later, walking home through the falling snow, Dawn realized something had fundamentally shifted. For the first time in years, she wasn't thinking about her exit strategy or calculating how long she could stay before restlessness set in.

She was thinking about what it would mean to build something, to choose somewhere, and to stop moving long enough to see what could grow.

She was thinking about staying.

The thought no longer terrified her. It felt like coming home.

Chapter 16:
The Snowball Gala

The next morning, the first thing she noticed was that she was smiling before she was fully awake, before memory could remind her whether she should or shouldn't be happy. Just pure, uncomplicated joy at being alive and being here.

Then she remembered: the gala, the snow, Thomas's hands on her waist as they danced, the whole town watching.

Her phone showed three messages from Thomas:

Good morning. Thank you for last night.

I know we have things to figure out, but I wanted you to know, yesterday was the best day I've had in years.

Coffee? If you're ready for public appearances with Holly Falls' most notorious billionaire.

Dawn laughed out loud. Actually laughed, alone in her bedroom, at 7:30 in the morning.

She texted back: *Busy Bean. 9 AM. Fair warning: Edna will probably interrogate you about your intentions.*

Looking forward to it.

The Busy Bean was exactly as crowded as Dawn expected it to be the morning after the gala, which meant it was completely packed with people who had opinions about last night and weren't shy about sharing them.

Thomas was already there when she arrived, sitting at a corner table with two coffee cups and a slightly shell-shocked expression, as if he'd just been thoroughly questioned by the Holly Falls breakfast crowd.

"How bad was it?" Dawn asked, sliding into the chair across from him.

"Mrs. Patterson asked if I was planning to 'make an honest woman' out of you. Mr. Hendricks wanted to know if Miller Enterprises was hiring. And Edna..." Thomas paused. "Edna asked whether my net worth included 'liquid assets' or was all 'tied up in stocks and whatnot.'"

"Oh no. You got the full treatment."

"I think I passed. It's hard to tell with Edna."

Dawn reached for her coffee and knocked it over, sending hot liquid across the table and onto Thomas's lap.

"Oh God, I'm so sorry—" She grabbed napkins, started dabbing at the spill, realized she was groping him in public, and sat back down hard. "I'm apparently not ready for public appearances."

Thomas was laughing, really laughing, the kind that made his eyes crinkle and his whole face light up.

"What's so funny?"

"You. This. The fact that last night we were dancing in front of the entire town like we had our lives figured out, and this morning you're attacking me with coffee."

"I didn't attack you. I had a small coffee failure."

"Is that what we're calling it?"

Dawn found herself laughing, too. The kind of helpless laughter that came from relief and happiness and the strange joy of discovering that someone could see you at your most ridiculous and still look at you as if you were exactly who they wanted to be sitting across from.

They cleaned up the coffee. Got another cup. Settled into the easy conversation that had been building between them for weeks, the kind where pauses felt comfortable, interruptions felt natural, and everything seemed funnier than it actually was.

It was perfect.

Until Thomas's phone started buzzing.

At first, he ignored it. Then he turned it face down on the table. Then he put it in his pocket. But it kept buzzing, short, insistent vibrations that cut through their conversation like a reminder of the world outside Holly Falls.

"You should probably take that," Dawn said after the fifth round of buzzing.

"It's fine. It can wait."

"Thomas."

"It's just work. Complications." His jaw tightened slightly. "Nothing that can't wait an hour."

But when it buzzed again immediately, Dawn saw something shift in his expression. Resignation, maybe, or recognition that the outside world had found him.

"I should probably..." He gestured at his pocket apologetically.

"Take it. I'll be here."

Thomas stepped outside to take the call, and Dawn watched him through the coffee shop window. She saw the exact moment he transformed from the man who'd laughed at her coffee attack into someone else entirely.

His posture changed. Shoulders squared. Jaw set. His free hand moved in gestures she didn't recognize, sharp, decisive movements that belonged in boardrooms and conference calls, not small-town breakfast dates.

This wasn't the Thomas who'd tangled Christmas lights or worn her father's sweatshirt as if it were designed specifically for him. This was CEO Thomas. Billionaire Thomas. The man who ran a company worth more than Holly Falls' entire annual budget.

When he came back inside, he was present in body but somewhere else entirely in mind.

"Everything okay?" Dawn asked.

"Fine. Just complications." The word sounded hollow the second time. "Where were we?"

They tried to pick up their conversation, but something had shifted. Thomas was distracted, answering questions a beat too late, his attention split between her and whatever crisis demanded his attention three states away.

After another round of buzzing, Dawn put her hand over his.

"Go," she said. "Handle whatever needs handling. We can do this later."

"I don't want to leave."

"I know. But your phone is about to vibrate itself off the table, and you keep looking at it like someone might be bleeding to death while we talk about coffee preferences."

Thomas squeezed her hand. "This isn't how I wanted this morning to go."

"I know. But we'll have other mornings."

He left. Dawn sat alone at their table, watching him walk away with his phone already to his ear, and felt the first shadow of doubt creep across her perfect morning.

That evening, Amy knocked on Dawn's bedroom door, wearing an expression Dawn had learned to associate with bad news.

"Have you been online today?"

"No. Why would I torture myself with the internet when I could be basking in the post-gala afterglow?"

Amy held out her phone. "You need to see this."

The headline made Dawn's stomach drop:

MILLER ENTERPRISES CEO'S HOLIDAY ROMANCE: Inside Thomas Miller's Small-Town Getaway and the Local Artist Who Caught His Eye

The article was thorough. Photos from the gala, Dawn in her blue dress, Thomas in his suit, both of them looking at each other as if they were the only people in the room. Photos of Dawn from her social media, her photography website, and the community center's promotional materials.

A timeline of Thomas's "sabbatical." Quotes from "sources close to the family" expressing concern about the CEO's "extended absence." Speculation about his "erratic behavior."

And then, the part that made Dawn feel sick:

"It's a charming story," says industry analyst Rebecca Vance, "but Miller Enterprises shareholders are growing nervous. The company's stock has dropped 3% since news of Miller's extended absence broke. The board is reportedly pressuring him to return to New York to address the Henderson acquisition before year-end, or risk losing the deal entirely."

Dawn scrolled further. There was more speculation about her "motives," about whether she'd known who Thomas was from the beginning, and about whether the romance was "genuine or strategic."

She felt like she was going to throw up.

"Dawn." Amy's voice was careful. "This is tabloid nonsense. You know that, right?"

"Is it? They have quotes, analysis, and sources."

"Sources who sell stories to business reporters."

"But the stock thing—" Dawn stared at the phone. "Amy, his company is losing money because I'm here instead of there."

"That's not on you. That's his choice."

"Is it? Or is he just..." Dawn couldn't finish the sentence.

She thought about his phone buzzing at breakfast. The way his shoulders had tightened when he took the call. The tension she'd seen in his jaw when he said "complications" as if it were nothing.

He'd known. He'd known about the stock drop, the board pressure, and the deal that was falling apart. And he hadn't told her.

Again.

Dawn picked up her phone and texted: *We need to talk. Now.*

Thomas called instead of texting back.

"What's wrong?" he asked, but she could hear in his voice that he already knew.

"Did you see the article?"

Silence. Then: "Which one?"

"The one about your 'holiday romance' and how your company's stock is tanking because you're here instead of doing your job."

More silence. "Dawn—"

"Were you going to tell me, or were you just going to keep pretending everything was fine while your board pressured you to leave?"

"It's not that simple—"

"Then explain it to me. Right now, it feels like you're hiding things again, and we literally talked about honesty twelve hours ago."

She heard him exhale. "The Henderson deal is falling apart. My board wants me in New York. And yes, the stock dropped because the market doesn't like uncertainty." A pause. "But that's not your fault. That's mine. For not being where I'm supposed to be."

"Where you're supposed to be." Dawn's voice was flat. "And where's that? New York? Running your empire?"

"I don't—I don't know." He sounded exhausted. "I thought I had more time. To figure things out. To see if this—if we—"

"If we're worth losing millions of dollars?"

"That's not what I said."

"That sounds like where it was heading."

They were both quiet. Dawn could hear him breathing and feel the distance between them suddenly become enormous, despite the fact that he was probably less than a mile away.

"I'm coming over," Thomas said.

"No." Dawn's voice was sharper than she intended. "I need to think. I need you to be honest with me right now. What are you going to do?"

The silence stretched so long she thought the call had dropped.

"I don't know," he said finally. "But I know I can't keep doing this. Pretending the two lives don't exist. Pretending I can have Holly Falls without losing everything I've built."

"So you're leaving."

"I didn't say that."

"But you're thinking it."

He didn't deny it.

Dawn closed her eyes. The hope from this morning felt very far away.

189

"I think we should take a step back," she said.

"Dawn—"

"I'm not saying it's over. I'm saying I need to figure out whether this is real. And I can't do that while you're deciding whether I'm worth your stock price."

"That's not fair."

"Maybe not. But it's how I feel." She swallowed hard. "Goodnight, Thomas."

She hung up before he could respond.

Dawn sat on her bed, phone in her hands, staring at nothing. She should have known. Should have seen it coming. Of course, there was a real world out there, a world where Thomas was responsible for thousands of employees, billions of dollars, and decisions that affected real people's lives. She'd been fooling herself into thinking that could just... pause. For her.

Amy knocked and came in without waiting for permission.

"Can I sit?"

Dawn nodded.

Amy settled next to her on the bed. "I told him to leave," Dawn said. "Not in so many words, but I basically told him to go back to New York."

"Is that what you want?"

"I don't know what I want." Dawn's voice cracked. "I want him to stay. But I also want him to be honest with me. He keeps choosing to protect me from things instead of trusting me to handle them."

"That's... not the worst flaw a person could have."

"It feels like a big one." Dawn pulled her knees to her chest. "What if the analysts are right? What if I'm just a distraction, a nice story he can tell himself while his real life falls apart?"

"Do you believe that?"

Dawn thought of Thomas at the bake sale, covered in flour and looking bewildered. Thomas on the ice rink, grabbing the railing as if his life depended on it. Thomas looking at her as if she hung the moon, even when she was being unreasonable.

"No," she said. "But I'm scared to trust what I believe."

"That's the whole thing, though, isn't it?" Amy put an arm around her. "Love is trusting someone when you don't have proof. When it would be easier not to."

"You make it sound simple."

"It's not. It's the hardest thing in the world." Amy squeezed her. "But sometimes the hardest things are the ones worth doing."

Dawn leaned against her sister. Outside, snow began to fall again, the same snow that had felt magical last night now seemed like a curtain coming down on something that had been too good to be real.

Somewhere across town, Thomas was making decisions about his future, about whether Holly Falls was worth fighting for or just a pleasant detour before he returned to his real life.

She hoped his choice wasn't goodbye. But she wasn't sure she'd blame him if it were.

The weight of two billion dollars, thousands of employees, and boardrooms full of people questioning his judgment was real in a way that small-town Christmas magic and unexpected love couldn't compete with.

Dawn only hoped love could be real enough to matter.

Chapter 17:
The Return

Thomas didn't sleep. He lay in his room at the Holly Falls Inn, staring at the ceiling and replaying Dawn's voice from their phone call. *I need you to be honest with me. Right now, what are you going to do?*

He had been honest. He'd told her he didn't know what to do. That was the most honest he'd been about anything in months.

The problem was that not knowing wasn't good enough. Not for Dawn. Not for his board. Not for the thousands of people whose jobs depended on the decisions he made in boardrooms hundreds of miles away.

His phone was full of messages he hadn't answered. Marcus, his assistant, increasingly urgent: *The board wants an emergency call tomorrow. Henderson's lawyers are threatening to walk. Stock down another 2% in after-hours trading. They need to know your timeline.*

Eric Sterling had texted once: *Whatever you're deciding, decide it properly. Half-measures help no one.*

And Dawn. Nothing from Dawn. Which was somehow worse than anything else.

At 4 AM, he gave up on sleep. He sat by the window and watched Holly Falls sleep under its blanket of snow and Christmas lights. Three weeks ago, he'd come here to escape, to find out who he was without the money, the pressure, the endless obligations.

He'd found her instead.

And now he had to decide whether loving her meant staying or going.

Eric Sterling knocked at 7 AM, dressed for travel, wearing a coat and scarf, the efficient look of someone who had a plane to catch and decisions to make.

"I'm heading back to New York," Eric said, settling into the chair by the window. "But I wanted to see you first."

"To tell me to come with you?"

"To see where your head's at." Eric's expression was serious. "The board is circling. You know that. Henderson is leverage. They'll use it to question your judgment, your focus, and whether you're fit to lead."

"I'm aware."

"Are you? Because from where I'm sitting, you're a man trying to live two lives, and you're about to lose them both."

Thomas didn't have a response to that. It was too accurate.

"What do you want, Thomas? Not what your father wanted. Not what the board wants. What do you truly want?"

Thomas looked out the window. He could see the town square from here, the Christmas tree, the bench where Dawn had sat the night she'd told Amy about his lie, and the gazebo where they'd shared their first kiss.

"I want her," he said quietly. "I want this place. I want to wake up without immediately calculating which fire to put out first."

"And?"

"And I know I can't have it. Not the way I want it." He turned to face Eric. "If I stay here, the company suffers. Real people lose their jobs. Deals fall apart. Stock prices drop. That's not hypothetical; that's math."

"And if you leave?"

"Then I lose her. Probably." Thomas ran his hands through his hair. "But at least I'm not dragging her into my mess. At least she can have a clean break."

"A clean break." Eric's voice was careful. "Is that what she wants?"

"I don't know what she wants. She told me to figure out if she's worth my stock price."

"And is she?"

Thomas laughed, but there was no humor in it. "She's worth more than all of it. Every dollar. Every share. That's the problem. I'd burn it all down for her if I could. But I can't. It's not just mine to burn."

Eric was quiet for a long moment.

"Your father," he said finally, "spent his whole life protecting the company at the expense of everything else. His marriage. His health. His relationship with you."

"I know."

"Do you want to make the same choice?"

"No. But I don't know how to make a different one."

Eric stood, placing a hand on Thomas's shoulder. "Figure it out before it's too late." He paused at the door. "And Thomas? Whatever you decide, make sure it's your decision. Not hers. Not the board's. Yours."

After Eric left, Thomas sat alone with the weight of everything he couldn't reconcile.

The board call took place at noon Eastern, 11 AM in Holly Falls. Thomas took it in his room, dressed in a suit for the first time since arriving, except for the gala. He looked like a stranger in the mirror, the CEO version of himself, polished and controlled.

The call was brutal.

"The Henderson deal needs to close by year-end, or the tax advantages will disappear," the chairman said. "Shareholder confidence is wavering. They need to see leadership."

"Your absence has been noted," another voice added. "Questions are being asked about your... focus."

Thomas listened. He responded when necessary. He didn't defend himself because there was nothing to defend. They were right. He had been absent. He had been focused elsewhere.

He'd been happy.

"We need you in New York by the twenty-sixth," the chairman continued. "The Henderson team has agreed to a final meeting. If you're not there, we lose the deal. And if we lose the deal..."

The implication was clear. They'd push for a vote of no confidence. His own board is turning against him.

"I'll be there," Thomas said.

The words came out before he'd fully decided, but once they were spoken, they were real.

"Excellent. We'll send the briefing materials this afternoon."

The call ended. Thomas sat in his suit, in his small inn room, and realized he had just chosen.

He was going back to New York.

Thomas tried to call Dawn. She didn't answer.

He texted: *Can we talk? Please.*

Nothing.

He walked to her house and knocked. Patricia answered, her expression wary but not hostile.

"She's not here," Patricia said. "She took her camera and went out. Said she needed to think."

"Do you know where—"

"I don't. Even if I did..." Patricia trailed off. "She needs space right now, Thomas. Whatever happened between you two, she needs time to process."

"I understand." He hesitated. "Can you tell her I came by? That I wanted to talk?"

"I'll tell her."

He walked back to the inn, barely noticing the busy town square full of last-minute Christmas shoppers and families enjoying their holiday week.

Back in his room, he sat at the small desk and took out the inn's stationery. If he couldn't talk to her, he'd write. He owed her that much.

The words came slowly at first, then faster.

Dawn,

I tried to call and came by your house. You're avoiding me, and I understand why. I haven't earned the right to ask for your time.

But I need you to know what I've decided, and I need you to know why.

I'm leaving tomorrow morning. The company needs me in New York, and I don't know how long it will take to stabilize things. Days. Weeks. Maybe longer.

I know what you're thinking. That I'm choosing money over you, that's not what this is.

I'm leaving because I can't ask you to build a life with someone who's always being pulled elsewhere. Because every time my phone rings, I become someone you didn't sign up for. Because loving you means wanting the best for you, and right now, I'm not sure I'm it.

You asked me to figure out whether you're worth my stock price. You're worth everything. That's why I have to go.

I can't be the person who asks you to make yourself smaller to fit into my complicated life. I can't be the reason you stop believing in the things that make you who you are.

You once said you're afraid of losing yourself when you stay somewhere. I'm afraid of you losing yourself if you stay with me.

I know this isn't what you want to hear. I know it probably feels like another lie, another way to protect you from a choice you should get to make. Maybe it is. But it's the only way I know to love you without ruining you.

Find your way home, Dawn. You don't need me for that. You never did. You just needed to stop running long enough to realize you were already there.

I'm sorry. For the lies. For the timing. For falling in love with you, knowing on some level it would end this way.

But I'm not sorry for these three weeks. They were the best three weeks of my life.

Thomas

P.S. The compass is yours. You'll know what to do with it.

Thomas folded the letter. Walked back to the Donovan house as the afternoon light was fading. Knocked again.

Patricia answered. She took one look at his face and knew.

"You're leaving."

"Yes."

"Does she know?"

He handed her the letter. "She will."

Patricia studied his face. "My daughter has spent her life running from what scares her. People who try to make decisions for her don't tend to last long."

"I'm not making a decision for her. I'm making one for me."

"Are you sure about that?"

He wasn't. But he nodded anyway.

"Goodbye, Mrs. Donovan. Thank you for welcoming me into your home."

He walked away before she could respond.

Dawn came home after dark. She'd been walking for hours, taking photos of nothing and avoiding her phone and her thoughts with equal determination.

Her mother was waiting in the kitchen.

"Thomas came by. Twice."

"I know. I saw the texts."

"He left this." Patricia handed her the letter. "I think you should read it now."

Something in her mother's voice made Dawn's stomach drop.

She took the letter. Went up to her room. Sat on her bed.

Opened it.

The first line hit her like a physical blow.

I'm leaving. Tomorrow morning.

She read the rest. Every word. Then read it again because it couldn't possibly mean what she thought it meant.

I'm leaving because loving you means wanting the best for you, and right now, I'm not sure I'm it.

He wasn't choosing the money over her. He was choosing to step back. To sacrifice what he wanted because he thought it was better for her. The noble idiot. The absolute fool.

She thought about all the times she'd run. All the times she'd convinced herself that leaving was protecting the people she left behind.

It wasn't. It was cowardice masquerading as kindness.

And now Thomas was doing the same thing.

She looked at Harold the Reindeer, who was still perched on her pillow.

"He's an idiot," she told Harold.

Harold offered no response.

"I'm going to have to chase him, aren't I?"

Harold stared with his unhinged eyes.

"I'm going to chase a billionaire to a train station on Christmas Eve. That's my life now."

She stood. Grabbed her coat.

She was done running. Which meant she was about to start chasing.

Dawn came downstairs. Her mother was still in the kitchen, pretending not to have been waiting.

"I need to borrow Dad's truck."

Patricia didn't ask why. She just handed over the keys.

"He said he was leaving tomorrow morning. What time?"

"I don't know."

"Then you should probably hurry."

Dawn was halfway out the door when her mother's voice stopped her.

"Dawn."

200

"Yeah?"

"Don't let him make this decision for you. That's not how love works."

Dawn nodded. Then she was gone, into the snow, toward whatever lay ahead.

Outside, the snow was falling harder now. It was Christmas Eve in Holly Falls, and somewhere in this small town, Thomas Miller was preparing to leave the best thing that had ever happened to him because he believed it was the right thing to do.

Dawn had spent her entire adult life running from complicated situations. Now she was about to find out what happened when she ran toward one instead.

The truck's engine protested the cold, but it started. Dawn pulled out of the driveway and into the snowy streets, headlights cutting through the darkness.

She had a billionaire to catch.

Chapter 18:
The Chase

D awn's hands were shaking on the steering wheel. Her father's truck was old, older than she was, and it protested the cold with groans and rattles that usually made her slow down. Tonight she didn't slow down.

The streets of Holly Falls were quiet on Christmas Eve. Everyone was inside with their families, warm lights glowing in windows, the kind of peaceful evening that belonged to other people's lives. Dawn blew through a stop sign, muttered an apology to no one, and kept driving.

The train station first. Thomas was leaving tomorrow morning, but she didn't know what that meant. Six AM? Seven? The Holly Falls station was tiny, barely more than a platform and a ticket booth, but it connected to the regional line to Indianapolis, from which she could go anywhere.

She should have asked. Should have demanded details instead of hanging up on him.

The platform was empty. The station was locked up for the holiday. A departure board showed the next train: 6:15 AM to Indianapolis.

He wasn't here. But he also hadn't left yet.

Dawn stood on the empty platform, breathing hard, and realized she had no idea where else to look.

Where would Thomas go on Christmas Eve? Where would someone sit to think about leaving everything behind?

The inn. She drove there first, but his car wasn't in the parking lot.

Her house, but he wouldn't go back there, not after delivering the letter.

The gazebo where they'd shared their first kiss. She ran to the town square, hope and desperation mixing in her chest, but the gazebo was empty except for the mistletoe still hanging from the ceiling.

The community center where they'd spent so many hours planning the gala. Dark and locked.

The Busy Bean. Closed.

Dawn leaned against the gazebo railing, breathing hard. She was running out of ideas, running out of places to search, running out of time.

Then her phone rang.

"Where are you?" Amy demanded.

"Town square. Looking for Thomas. He wasn't at the station."

"I know where he is."

Dawn's heart stuttered. "What? How?"

"Mom called Mrs. Mathers at the inn. She said his car is parked at the old Peterson barn, the one at the edge of town."

The Peterson barn. The one Dawn had told Thomas about during their bonfire conversation. Her dream studio. The place she'd imagined turning into something real.

"Why would he be there?"

"I don't know. But that's where his car is. Go."

Dawn turned the truck and headed for the barn.

The Peterson barn sat dark against the sky, its sagging roof dusted with snow. It had been empty for years, a beautiful ruin that Dawn had photographed dozens of times, always imagining what it could become.

Thomas's rental car was parked outside.

Dawn pulled up beside it and got out. The cold hit her immediately; she'd forgotten her gloves, her hat, everything except the need to find him.

The barn door stood ajar. Light spilled out, faint and flickering. Candles, maybe, or a lantern.

She pushed the door open.

Thomas was sitting on an old wooden crate in the center of the barn. The space was huge and hollow, filled with shadows and the smell of old hay. He'd lit a camping lantern, she had no idea where he'd gotten it, and he was looking at something on his phone.

He looked up when she entered. His whole face changed.

"Dawn?"

"You're a complete idiot."

Whatever he'd expected her to say, it wasn't that.

"I—what?"

"Your letter." She was walking toward him now, fury and relief and terror all tangled together. "You're leaving because you think it's better for me? You're removing yourself from my life because you've decided I deserve someone less complicated?"

"I was trying to—"

"I know what you were trying to do. You were trying to make my choices for me, which is exactly what you said you wouldn't do." She stopped in front of him. He was standing now, the lantern light catching the exhaustion on his face. "You don't get to decide what's best for me, Thomas. That's my job."

"Dawn, my life is. You saw the article. The board, the company, the constant—"

"I saw it. And I don't care."

"You should care. You deserve better than—"

"Stop." Her voice was sharp enough to make him stop talking. "Stop telling me what I deserve. Stop protecting me from things I didn't ask to be protected from. Stop being so afraid of hurting me that you hurt me anyway."

Thomas was silent. His hands gripped his knees.

"Why are you here?" Dawn asked, softer now. "In this barn. Of all places."

He looked around at the sagging beams, the gaps in the roof where snow had drifted in, and the potential hiding under decades of neglect.

"You told me about it," he said. "Your dream. The studio you imagined. I wanted to see it."

"At midnight? On Christmas Eve?"

"I wanted to see if I could make it happen. As a—" He stopped. Swallowed hard. "As a gift. A goodbye gift. I was going to have my foundation buy it, restore it, and give it to you. So at least something good would come from all this."

Dawn stared at him. "You were going to buy me a building."

"I was going to try."

"As a goodbye present."

"I know how it sounds—"

"It sounds insane, Thomas. It sounds like something a character in a bad romance novel would do."

"I know."

"It sounds like you were going to throw money at a problem rather than actually talking to me about it."

"I know." His voice cracked. "I'm not good at this. Being a person instead of a CEO. Talking instead of fixing. You're the first person who's ever made me want to learn, and I keep getting it wrong."

The anger drained from Dawn. What was left was just—

Love. Exasperation. The overwhelming urge to shake him and kiss him, in equal measure.

"You're an idiot," she said again.

"You mentioned that already."

"A well-meaning, noble, and completely infuriating idiot."

"I'm getting that."

She stepped closer. Close enough to touch. Didn't touch him, not yet.

"You want to know what I actually want, not what you think I deserve. What I want."

"Yes."

"I want you. The messy version. The version with board calls and stock prices and complications. I want the guy who can't ice skate, learns to make pinecones, and looks at me like I'm the answer to a question he didn't know he was asking."

Thomas's eyes were bright. He didn't move.

"I want you to stay," Dawn continued. "But if you have to go to New York, I want you to come back. If you can't come back, I want to figure out how we make this work anyway. Because I'm done running from things that scare me, which means I need you to stop running too."

"Dawn—"

"I love you. Okay? I love you. Your letter said you love me, and if that's true, if any of it is true, then you don't get to leave without a fight."

The silence stretched. The barn creaked around them, the old wood settling in the cold.

"I was going to get on the train," Thomas said quietly. "Tomorrow morning. I had my bag packed. I was ready."

"And now?"

He took her hands. His fingers were cold, yet his grip was steady.

"And now I'm standing in a falling-down barn with the woman I love, and she's telling me I'm an idiot, and I think—" His voice broke. "I think maybe being an idiot isn't the worst thing in the world, if it means I get to be her idiot."

Dawn laughed. It came out as a half-sob.

"That's the worst line I've ever heard."

"I'm aware."

"You should be embarrassed."

"I am. Deeply."

She kissed him.

The first touch of her lips against his was soft, almost tentative—but only for a heartbeat. Then Dawn pressed closer, her hands sliding up to frame his face, and Thomas made a sound that was half relief, half surrender.

This wasn't like the mistletoe kiss—tentative, testing. This wasn't like the gala kiss—complicated, weighted with everything left unsaid.

This was about two people who'd stopped running. Two people who'd decided, against all reason, to stay.

Thomas's arms came around her waist, pulling her against him until there was no space between them, until he could feel her heartbeat against his chest. Dawn's fingers tangled in his hair, longer than when they'd first met, curling slightly at the edges from the cold, and she kissed him more deeply.

She tasted like snow and the faint sweetness of her mother's Christmas cookies. Thomas had kissed other women, but this, Dawn arching against him in a falling-down barn, her hands sure and demanding on his skin, was different. This was everything he'd been too afraid to want and too stupid to ask for.

When Dawn's teeth caught his bottom lip, just a gentle tug that made his knees forget how to hold him up, Thomas thought dimly that he would have gladly spent the rest of his life as this particular kind of idiot if it meant she kept kissing him as if he were her last breath of air.

His hands found the small of her back, the patch of warm skin where her sweater had ridden up, and Dawn shivered against him, not from cold, but from the way his thumbs traced small circles there. She broke the kiss just long enough to breathe his name against his mouth, and the sound of it, soft and wondering and completely wrecked, nearly undid him.

"Dawn," he whispered back, and kissed the corner of her mouth, her cheek, and the sensitive spot just below her ear, making her fingers tighten in his hair.

She pulled back enough to look at him, her eyes bright and wide in the lantern light. Her lips were swollen from his kisses, her hair spilling from its braid in ways that made him want to bury his hands in it and never let go.

"Say it again," she said, her voice rough. "Tell me you love me. Not in a letter. Not in a goodbye. Right here."

Thomas cupped her face in his hands, his thumbs tracing the line of her cheekbones. "I love you, Dawn Donovan. I love your terrible packing skills and the way you talk to Harold the Reindeer as if he's going to answer. I love that you run toward things when you're scared instead of away from them. I love that you came after me tonight, even though I gave you every reason not to."

Dawn's eyes filled with tears. "I love you too, even though you're an idiot who thinks buying someone a building is an appropriate romantic gesture."

"In my defense, you really liked the building."

She laughed, and the sound was so bright and real and purely Dawn that Thomas had to kiss her again, had to taste that laughter on her lips and commit it to memory. This time, when they kissed, it was slower, sweeter— a conversation instead of a claim, a promise instead of a plea.

When they finally broke apart, they were both breathing hard, their foreheads pressed together in the flickering lantern light.

"I'm still angry at you," Dawn said.

"Fair."

"You can't just decide to leave without talking to me first."

"I know. I'm sorry."

"And you definitely can't buy me a building as a goodbye present."

"What about as a staying present?"

She stared at him. "Thomas."

"I'm serious. Not as a gift, as a project. Something we do together. I have the resources. You have the vision." He gestured toward the barn around them. "This place could be amazing. You said so yourself."

"I said it was a stupid dream."

"You said a lot of things. Most of them were lies you told yourself because you were scared." He touched her face. "I know about lying to yourself because you're scared. I'm an expert at it."

Dawn looked around the barn. Really looked. At the high ceilings and the good bones beneath the decay. At the potential hiding beneath years of neglect.

"It would be a lot of work," she said.

"I like work. When it's the right kind of work."

"It would be expensive."

"I have money. More than I know what to do with, remember?"

"It would be a commitment. Long-term. Staying in one place."

"I know." Thomas's smile was uncertain but real. "Terrifying, isn't it?"

Dawn kissed him again. Softer this time. Like a promise.

"What about your board? The Henderson deal?"

"I'll go back to New York. I'll handle what needs handling. But I'll come back." He pulled her closer. "I'll always come back. If you want me to."

"I want you to."

"Even if it's messy? Even if it takes time to figure out?"

"Especially then." Dawn leaned into him. "I'm done with easy, Thomas. Easy is boring. Easy is safe. I want complicated. I want real."

They stood together in the falling-down barn, surrounded by the smell of old hay and the promise of something new. Outside, snow fell harder now, covering Holly Falls in Christmas Eve quiet.

"So, what happens now?" Thomas asked.

"Now we go home. You unpack your bag. We have Christmas with my family if you want."

"I want."

"And then we figure out how to make this work. The company, the town, this place. All of it."

"Together?"

"Together."

They gathered the lantern and walked back to their cars. Dawn's father's truck started reluctantly, its headlights cutting through the snow. Thomas's rental purred to life behind her.

She pulled out first, watching him follow in her rearview mirror, not running away this time. Both of them are heading home.

Tomorrow would bring complications, board calls, business pressures, and all the practical realities of building a life that spanned two worlds. But tonight, Christmas Eve in Holly Falls, they had each other, a plan, and a falling-down barn full of possibilities.

It was enough. It was everything.

Dawn drove through the snowy streets toward home, toward family, toward the first Christmas in years that felt like a beginning rather than an ending.

In her rearview mirror, Thomas's headlights followed steadily and surely. He wasn't running either.

They'd both finally stopped running and started building something worth staying for.

Chapter 19:
True North

They pulled up to the Donovan house just before midnight on Christmas Eve. The lights were still on, every light, it looked like, the house blazing like a beacon against the snow. Amy's car was in the driveway, and so was Will's truck.

"They waited up," Dawn said.

"Should I be worried?"

"Probably."

Thomas exhaled slowly. "I deserve whatever's coming."

"You do. But they'll be nice about it. Eventually."

They got out of their cars. Dawn reached for Thomas's hand, deliberately and visibly. If they were doing this, they were doing it properly.

The front door opened before they reached it.

Patricia Donovan stood in the doorway, wearing a bathrobe and an unreadable expression. Behind her, Dawn could see Amy hovering and Doug standing back with his arms crossed.

"Well," Patricia said. "You found him."

"I found him."

"And?"

Dawn looked at Thomas, and Thomas looked at Dawn.

"And we have a lot to figure out," Dawn said. "But we're figuring it out together."

Patricia's expression didn't change for a long moment. Then she stepped aside.

"Good," she said simply. "Come inside. It's cold."

The kitchen became an impromptu tribunal. Patricia served hot chocolate while Doug asked questions with the methodical patience of someone who'd raised two daughters and knew how to get information.

"You're the billionaire who lied to my daughter," Doug said. It wasn't a question.

"Yes, sir," Thomas replied.

"Do you love her?"

"More than I've ever loved anything."

"Good answer." Doug studied him over his mug. "Are you going to hurt her again?"

"I'm going to try not to. But I'm probably going to mess up. I'm not good at this."

"What, specifically?"

"Being in love. Being a person instead of a company. Talking instead of fixing things with money." Thomas met Doug's eyes. "Your daughter is teaching me. I'm a slow learner, but I'm motivated."

Amy snorted. "That might be the most honest thing anyone's ever said in this kitchen."

The clock in the hallway chimed midnight. Doug raised his mug.

"To family," he said. "However it grows."

They all drank. Thomas looked like he might cry.

"All right, everyone, let's say goodnight. It is already Christmas, but let's all get some sleep," said Doug.

Dawn woke to the smell of cinnamon and the sound of voices downstairs. It was Christmas morning, the first in years that felt like something to celebrate rather than something to endure.

She pulled on her robe and padded down to find chaos in the kitchen. Thomas was at the stove, attempting pancakes, while Patricia coached from one side and Amy provided running commentary from the other.

"No, flip them now—no, wait—okay, that one's definitely going to—" Patricia reached for the spatula.

"I've got it," Thomas said, but he very clearly didn't have it.

"They're abstract art," Amy observed. "Very modern. Very... burnt."

Thomas looked up when Dawn entered. His hair was sticking up, he had flour on his shirt, and he looked more relaxed than she had ever seen him.

"I'm making breakfast," he announced.

"How's that going?" Dawn asked.

"Badly. But with enthusiasm."

Patricia actually laughed and took the spatula from him. "Go sit. I'll finish these."

"I wanted to help."

"You are helping. By not burning down my kitchen."

After breakfast, they gathered around the tree. The tradition was simple: everyone received one ornament for the tree, something that represented the year. Patricia had been doing it since the girls were small.

Amy went first, with a tiny picture frame featuring a photo of her and Will from their engagement party. Will got a fishing lure because, apparently, that's what made him happy.

Doug presented Patricia with a small glass angel, and she gave him a miniature snow globe of the town square.

Then Patricia turned to Thomas.

"Every family member gets one," she said, holding out a carefully wrapped box.

Thomas took it as if it might explode. Opened it slowly.

Inside was a glass snowflake, delicate, hand-blown, catching the light from the tree.

"Patricia," Thomas said, his voice rough. "I don't—"

"You're here," Patricia said simply. "That's enough."

Thomas held the ornament as if it were the most precious thing he'd ever owned, which Dawn realized it might be. He hung it on the tree with unsteady hands.

At noon, Thomas's phone rang. He glanced at it, apologized, and stepped outside to answer the call.

Dawn watched from the window as he paced on the porch, talking with his hands. When he came back in, he looked relieved.

"Eric," he explained. "The Henderson situation will keep until the twenty-seventh."

"Your lawyer called you on Christmas?" Amy asked.

"Eric's not just my lawyer. He's—" Thomas paused. "He's the closest thing to family I had before this."

"Had?" Doug asked.

Thomas looked around the room, at Patricia cleaning up wrapping paper, at Amy and Will curled up on the couch, and at Dawn curled up in the armchair with Harold the Reindeer.

"Have," he corrected. "He's the closest thing I had before I found you."

After lunch, Dawn and Thomas walked into town. She wanted to show him Holly Falls on Christmas Day, with quiet streets, families visible through windows, and the peaceful aftermath of celebration.

They ran into Mayor Posey coming out of the church.

"Dawn, Thomas." She smiled genuinely. "Merry Christmas."

"Merry Christmas," Dawn replied.

"I trust you've both had time to consider our conversation about community development proposals."

Dawn blinked. "What conversation?"

"The Peterson property," Mayor Posey continued smoothly. "Mrs. Peterson is quite interested in seeing it go to someone local, someone invested in the community." She looked meaningfully between them. "I believe I mentioned it might be available?"

Dawn looked at Thomas. Thomas looked back.

"We'll be in touch," Thomas said.

Mayor Posey nodded and continued on her way, leaving them standing on the snowy sidewalk.

"Did we just get the mayor's blessing to buy a barn?" Thomas asked.

"I think we did."

"This town is insane."

"You love it."

"I do." He took her hand. "I love all of it."

They walked through the square, past the gazebo where they'd had their first kiss, past the fountain where she'd made her wish. People waved from windows, called Christmas greetings from doorways. The response had shifted, warm, curious, accepting.

This was what belonging felt like. Not just being tolerated, but being claimed.

That evening, Dawn slipped out to the porch. The day had been wonderful, overwhelming in the best way, but she needed a quiet moment.

The snow was falling again, light flurries dusting the railings. The town was dark except for softly glowing Christmas lights in the distance.

She thought about her wish, the one she'd written on that scrap of paper and tucked into Nana's ornament weeks ago.

A place to land. Someone who won't make me stay.

She'd thought it was a contradiction. Two things that couldn't coexist.

But Thomas wasn't making her stay. He was giving her a reason to want to. The difference was everything.

The door opened behind her.

"You're going to freeze," Thomas said.

"I'm thinking."

"You can think inside."

"It's not the same." She made room for him on the porch railing. He joined her, shoulder to shoulder, looking out at the snow.

"What are you thinking about?"

"The wish I made. At the beginning of all this."

"What did you wish for?"

Dawn hesitated. She'd never told anyone, not even Amy.

"A place to land," she said finally. "And someone who won't make me stay. Or will go with me."

Thomas was quiet for a moment.

"Did it come true?"

She looked at him, this man who'd stumbled into her life carrying donation boxes, who'd learned to wire pinecones, and who'd tried to leave but couldn't.

"I think it did," she said. "I think you're it."

His arm came around her. She leaned into him, and they sat together on the porch, watching the snow fall over Holly Falls.

"I have something for you," Thomas said.

"I thought you didn't have a gift."

"I didn't, but I found something." He reached into his pocket and pulled out a small object.

It was a compass. Old brass, weathered with age, fitting perfectly in his palm.

"I found it in the barn," he said. "Buried in one of the old toolboxes. I don't know how long it's been there, but—" He opened it, revealing the inside to her.

Someone had scratched words into the metal, faded but legible: *Find your way home*.

"I thought it was appropriate," Thomas said. "For someone who spent years running and someone who's finally ready to stay."

Dawn took the compass. It was heavier than it looked. The needle swung, then settled, pointing north, toward the dark shape of the Peterson barn on the edge of town.

"This is real," she said. "We're really doing this."

"We're really doing this."

"It's going to be complicated."

"I know."

"You're going to have to go to New York sometimes."

"I know."

"And I'm going to have to learn what it means to stay in one place."

"We will stay here from time to time, visit New York occasionally, and sometimes take trips abroad to explore different places. We'll figure it out." He took her hand, the compass cool between their palms. "Together."

Dawn looked at the compass. At Thomas. At the town she'd been so afraid to call home.

"Together," she agreed.

Inside, the house was warm and loud, with Amy and Will playing some kind of card game that involved a lot of arguing, and her parents cleaning up the kitchen while bickering good-naturedly about dishwasher-loading techniques.

Family. The messy, wonderful, complicated kind she'd spent years running from.

The kind she finally understood was worth staying for.

Thomas squeezed her hand as they walked back into the warmth.

"Thank you," he said quietly.

"For what?"

"For chasing me. For not letting me be an idiot. For showing me what home looks like."

Dawn kissed him softly, there in the doorway between the cold night and the warm house, between her old life of running and her new life of staying put. She snuggled into his warmth, loving the feel of his arms around her.

"Thank you for being worth chasing."

They went inside, to the noise and the laughter and the family that had grown by one today.

The wish was fulfilled. Everything else—the barn, the company, the logistics of loving someone across state lines and tax brackets—was just detail.

Details they'd figure out together.

The compass in Dawn's pocket pointed north, toward the future they were going to build.

She couldn't wait to get started.

Chapter 20:
The Final Dance

December 26th arrived with the gentle quiet that always followed Christmas, the peaceful aftermath of celebration, when wrapping paper had been cleared and presents found their places in daily life. The food that was consumed to send you into a coma on the couch, pretending to watch football.

Dawn woke thinking about the Peterson barn.

It was becoming a habit, this morning ritual of imagining the space transformed. In her mind, the sagging roof had been repaired, the red walls freshly painted, the interior cleared and divided into studios. She could see it so clearly: easels by the windows, pottery wheels in the corner, a photography darkroom in the back, and space for community workshops and children's art classes.

"You're thinking about the barn again," Thomas said from beside her.

"How do you know?"

"You get this look. Like you're building something in your head."

"I am building something in my head."

"Good." He turned to face her, propping himself up on his elbow. "I called Mrs. Peterson yesterday."

Dawn's eyes snapped open. "You what?"

"I called, introduced myself properly, and mentioned that we might be interested in discussing the property."

"Thomas—"

"She invited us for tea tomorrow at three o'clock." His smile was uncertain. "I hope that was okay. I know we haven't discussed specifics yet, but—"

Dawn kissed him. Right there in her childhood bed, with the glow-in-the-dark stars still stuck to her ceiling and her parents probably already awake downstairs.

"It's more than okay," she said against his mouth. "It's perfect."

The Holly Falls Day-After-Christmas Potluck was a tradition that had evolved organically over decades. Someone, Dawn had never discovered who, had started it to use up holiday leftovers and extend the celebration by one more day. Now it was as much a part of the season as Christmas itself.

The community center was transformed from its gala elegance into comfortable chaos. Folding tables covered with mismatched dishes, kids running between legs, the sound of laughter and argument, and holiday music from someone's ancient boombox.

Dawn and Thomas arrived together, carrying Patricia's green bean casserole and Doug's famous mac and cheese. This was deliberate, another public statement, another choice to stop hiding.

The reaction was exactly what Dawn had hoped for. Warm, curious, and accepting.

Mrs. Patterson, who'd been suspicious of Thomas since the billionaire revelation, complimented his tie. Mr. Hendricks wanted to discuss a community poetry series for the arts center. Even Edna Morrison, the queen of the pie competition, asked whether he'd be judging next year's contest.

"You're good at this," Dawn murmured, watching Thomas endure a twenty-minute conversation about the historical significance of Holly Falls' original town charter.

"Good at what?"

"Being normal. Fitting in."

"I'm not fitting in. I'm just—" He paused, considering. "I'm being myself. The self I found here."

Mayor Posey intercepted them near the dessert table.

"Thomas. Dawn. I trust you've had time to discuss our conversation regarding the Peterson property?"

"We're meeting with Mrs. Peterson tomorrow," Thomas said.

"Excellent. She's quite interested in seeing it go to someone local, someone invested in the community." Mayor Posey's smile was genuinely warm. "She saw you there on Christmas Eve, apparently. Said you looked at the place like you could see what it could become."

"We can," Dawn said.

"Good. Holly Falls needs more dreamers who actually build things."

As the evening progressed, someone pushed the tables back, and someone else hooked up better speakers. The kids were corralled into a corner with leftover cookies, and the adults started dancing.

It wasn't elegant. It was clumsy and joyful and exactly what Dawn hadn't known she needed.

Thomas pulled her onto the makeshift dance floor.

"I'm warning you now, I'm still terrible at this," he said.

"I remember." Dawn let him lead her into what was generously called a waltz. "I don't care."

"You should. I'm about to step on your feet."

"Then step on them. We'll figure it out."

They danced—badly, wonderfully—while the community swirled around them. Dawn felt the weight of belonging, of choosing and being chosen in turn.

"I want this," Thomas said quietly, so only she could hear it.

"Dancing? Because you're getting better—"

"No. This." He gestured around them. "The potlucks. The meddling neighbors. I don't understand the traditions yet, but I want to learn. You." His voice was steady. "This isn't temporary for me, Dawn. This isn't some kind of sabbatical from my real life. This is what I want my life to look like."

Dawn's throat tightened. "What about New York? The company?"

"I'll figure it out. Remote management, strategic travel, and hiring people I trust to handle day-to-day operations." He spun her, badly, but enthusiastically. "My father spent forty years building something he thought would make him happy. I'd rather spend forty years building something I know will."

"And what's that?"

"A life with you. A marriage, eventually, if you'll have me. Kids running around the barn studio, getting paint on everything. A future that matters more than profit margins."

Dawn laughed, but her eyes were watery. "That sounds terrifying."

"Good terrifying or bad terrifying?"

"The best kind of terrifying."

As the evening wound down, they slipped away quietly. No dramatic exits, no announcements, just two people walking out into the snow, toward the edge of town where possibility waited.

Thomas had somehow procured blankets and a battery-powered lantern. Dawn didn't ask where or how. She was learning that Thomas approached problems with a particular kind of methodical determination, which usually resulted in solutions appearing as if by magic.

The barn was cold but sheltered, quiet except for the wind whistling through the gaps in the boards. They spread the blankets in the center of the space, lit the lantern, and sat together, looking at what could be.

"Tell me your vision," Thomas said. "All of it. The impractical parts, the expensive parts, the parts that make no business sense."

Dawn leaned back against his chest, looking up at the rafters. "Photography studio in the loft. Natural light from those windows. Pottery wheels down here, two or three, so we can offer classes. Easels for painting workshops. Maybe a small kiln in the back corner."

"Community access?"

"The membership will be on a sliding scale to accommodate different financial situations. We can also offer free workshops specifically for children to help engage young community members in the arts. We can also consider partnering with the school district to integrate art education into their programs. She looked at him carefully and added, "This isn't a profit-driven venture, Thomas. It's likely not even designed to break even financially."

"Good. I'm tired of everything being about money." He was quiet for a moment. "What would you call it?"

"I don't know. The Peterson Collective? Holly Falls Arts Center?" She laughed. "I'm terrible at naming things."

"We'll figure it out." Thomas's arms tightened around her. "We have time."

The conversation drifted, practical considerations and wild dreams mixing together like plans and wishes. Dawn found herself thinking about workshops she could teach, artists she could invite, and the kind of community space she'd always imagined but never dared to pursue.

"This is really happening," she said.

"If you want it to happen."

"I want it. I want all of it." Dawn turned in his arms to face him. "The barn, the collective, the complicated future with you. I want the version where I stay and build something instead of running away when things get hard."

"Even when things get hard?"

"Especially then."

Thomas cupped her face in his hands. "I love you."

"I love you too."

He kissed her, and it was different from the desperate kisses of Christmas Eve or the tentative ones of their early courtship. This was two people who'd chosen each other completely, who'd seen the worst in each other and decided to stay anyway.

Dawn's hands found the buttons of his shirt, fingers working with deliberate slowness. Each piece of clothing that fell away felt like another wall coming down, another barrier dissolving. Thomas's breath caught when her palms spread across his chest, mapping the landscape of him with reverent attention.

"Are you sure?" he whispered against her temple, even as his hands traced the curve of her spine through the soft wool of her sweater.

"I've never been more sure of anything," Dawn breathed back, and the certainty in her voice undid him.

They moved together with the unhurried exploration that came from knowing this wasn't goodbye, wasn't stolen time, wasn't secret. Thomas's mouth followed the path his hands had mapped, the hollow of her throat, the curve of her shoulder, the sensitive spot just above her collarbone that made her arch against him and whisper his name like a prayer.

Dawn had thought she knew desire before, but this was different. This was want without fear, need without the urge to flee. When Thomas's hands found the hem of her sweater and lifted it away, when his eyes darkened at the sight of her in the flickering lantern light, she felt beautiful instead of vulnerable.

"God, Dawn," Thomas murmured, his voice rough with wonder. "Look at you."

She pulled him down to her, skin meeting skin, warmth chasing away the barn's December chill. They had time now, all the time in the world, and they used it. No ticking clocks, no imminent departures, no secrets between them. Just Dawn and Thomas learning each other with the kind of patient thoroughness that spoke of forever, not just tonight.

Thomas worshipped her with his hands and mouth, drawing from her sounds she didn't know she could make, building tension until she trembled beneath him. Dawn returned every touch, every kiss, mapping the muscles of his shoulders and the sensitive spot behind his ear that made him groan her name.

When they finally came together, it was with the slow, sweet burn of recognition, two people who'd found their missing piece. Dawn's hands tangled in Thomas's hair as he moved above her, their foreheads pressed together, breathing the same air and watching each other's faces in the golden light.

"I love you," she whispered as the tension between them built, and Thomas answered by kissing her breathless, by holding her as if she were everything he'd ever wanted, by moving with her to the rhythm of two hearts finally beating in sync.

The intimacy that followed was tender and unhurried. They had time now to savor each touch, each sigh, each moment of connection that bound them closer. Just Dawn and Thomas, choosing each other in a falling-down barn that would become beautiful because they'd decided to build it together.

Afterward, they lay tangled in blankets, the lantern casting gentle shadows across the walls around them. Dawn's head rested on Thomas's chest, and his fingers combed slowly through her hair. She could hear his heartbeat gradually slow and feel the contentment radiating from him in waves that matched her own.

"No regrets?" Thomas asked softly, his voice still rough from their lovemaking.

Dawn lifted her head to look at him, taking in his tousled hair, the satisfied curve of his mouth, and the way he looked at her as if she'd hung the moon.

"Only that we waited this long," she said, and meant it.

"We should probably talk to Mrs. Peterson before we keep breaking in," Dawn said drowsily.

"Probably."

"And you should call your assistant. Let him know you're not coming back to New York yet."

"How long can you stay?" she'd asked.

"As long as you want me," he'd answered.

"Forever, then," Dawn murmured against his shoulder.

"Forever works for me."

They walked back to town as the sky began to lighten, Thomas's arm around Dawn's shoulders, their breath visible in the cold air. At the edge of the square, Thomas stopped.

"One more thing," he said, reaching into his pocket.

He pulled out a slightly crushed sprig of mistletoe, probably stolen from the potluck decorations.

"Where did you—"

"I appropriated it. Very subtly." He held it over her head. "For tradition."

Dawn laughed, rising on her toes to kiss him under the mistletoe in the middle of Holly Falls as the sun rose the day after Christmas.

"You know," she said, "a year ago I was running from everything that scared me. Now I'm kissing a billionaire under stolen mistletoe and planning to turn a barn into an art collective."

"How does that feel?"

Dawn looked around, at the town square she'd been afraid to call home, at the man who'd taught her the difference between being trapped and being rooted, and at the life she was finally brave enough to want.

"Like coming home," she said.

They walked the rest of the way hand in hand, past the gazebo where they'd had their first kiss, past the fountain where she'd made her wish, toward the house where her family was probably already awake and wondering where they'd been.

The wish had been fulfilled. The story was complete.

Everything else, including the barn renovation, the wedding planning, and the careful balance of Thomas's business life and their chosen small-town existence, was just the beginning.

The best kind of beginning: the kind you choose instead of the kind that chooses you.

Epilogue:
One Year Later

December 23rd. One year later. Dawn drove into Holly Falls as the sun set, painting the snow gold and pink. The town looked the same, with Christmas lights on every lamppost, wreaths on every door, and the big tree in the square glowing against the darkening sky.

But she was different.

She noticed it in small ways. The ease with which she took the familiar turns. The lack of escape routes ran through her mind. The way her hands didn't grip the steering wheel with the old restless energy that used to follow her everywhere.

Her phone buzzed. Thomas: *ETA?*

Dawn: *Ten minutes. Traffic on 31.*

Thomas: *Your mom started the cider without you. I tried to intervene. I failed.*

Dawn: *Did you at least save me the good cookies?*

Thomas: *I'm insulted you had to ask.*

She was smiling at her phone—still, after a year, smiling at her phone like a lovesick idiot—when she crested the hill and saw it.

The Peterson barn.

It wasn't the falling-down ruin she'd chased Thomas to last Christmas Eve. The roof had been repaired, and the walls had been painted deep red,

233

the color she'd chosen after six months of deliberation. The sign out front read: Holly Falls Arts Collective - Opening Spring 2026.

Dawn pulled over. Just for a moment. Just to look.

A year ago, this had been a dream she was too scared to say out loud. Now it was real. Permits filed, contractors hired, opening date set. Her photography studio on the upper level, community classroom space below, and sliding-scale programs funded by Thomas's foundation.

She pulled out her phone and took a picture. Not for social media or documentation, just for herself. Evidence of what happened when you stopped running long enough to build something worth staying for.

The Donovan house was ablaze with lights when she arrived, just as it had been the year before. But this time, she wasn't chasing anyone. This time, she was just coming home.

Thomas met her at the door before she could knock. He was wearing Doug's 1987 Indiana State sweatshirt, the same one he'd borrowed last Christmas and never returned. It had become his uniform for family gatherings, a badge of belonging that made Patricia smile whenever she saw it.

"You're late," he said, kissing her hello.

"I stopped to look at the barn."

"How's it looking?"

"Like a dream becoming real."

"Good." He helped her out of her coat. "Fair warning, Amy's on a mission tonight. She wants the proposal details."

"I told her the proposal story."

"You told her the bullet points. She wants the full romantic narrative." Thomas grinned. "Something about needing vicarious romance while she's pregnant with child number two."

234

Dawn looked over his shoulder into the living room, where Amy was holding court from the couch, one hand on her very pregnant belly.

"How is she?"

"Huge. Cranky. Demanding that Will rub her feet every twenty minutes." Thomas lowered his voice. "She's also ridiculously happy, but don't tell her I said that."

The next hour was a blur of food and family, the controlled chaos that defined Donovan Christmases. Thomas moved through it easily now. He helped Doug untangle the Christmas lights. He let Patricia feed him three different kinds of cookies while providing commentary on each one.

He belonged here, not as a guest, but as family.

Dawn caught herself watching him from across the room. She still did that sometimes, watching him as if she couldn't quite believe he was real or that this life was hers.

"Stop staring at your fiancé," Amy murmured, appearing beside her. "It's weird."

"I'm not staring."

"You're definitely staring. You've been staring for a year."

Dawn glanced down at her left hand, where the vintage engagement ring caught the light from the Christmas tree. Delicate filigree setting, a small diamond that looked as if it held starlight. Thomas had it designed by a jeweler in Vermont who specialized in antique reproductions. It was exactly her, understated, unusual, beautiful without trying too hard.

"Can you blame me?" Dawn asked.

"No," Amy said with a grin. "But you could be less obvious about it."

After dinner, they decorated the tree.

This was now tradition, different from before, expanded. Junior hung ornaments on the lowest branches with the intense concentration of someone performing surgery. Will held him up so he could reach the higher ones. Thomas had his own ornament, the glass snowflake from last year, given its own hook near the front of the tree.

Dawn found herself standing with Amy near the back of the room, watching the chaos.

"Do you remember last year?" Amy asked. "The wish ornament?"

Dawn remembered. The scrap of paper. The words she'd been too scared to say out loud. *A place to land. Someone who won't make me stay. Or will go with me.*

"I remember."

"Did you make a new wish this year?"

Dawn shook her head. "Didn't need to."

"Really?"

"The old one came true." She watched Thomas place a star at the top of the tree. "Everything I wished for. Everything I was afraid to want."

Amy was quiet for a moment. Then: "Tell me about the proposal. You never gave me the full story."

"I told you—"

"You gave me bullet points. I want details." Amy's hand rested on her belly. "I'm about to have my second child. I need romance vicariously."

Dawn laughed. But she settled against the wall, letting the memory surface.

"It was September. We were in France for a foundation event. Thomas had meetings, and I was doing photography for the annual report. Very glamorous, mostly boring boardrooms and hotel conference centers."

"Sounds thrilling."

"But on the last day, he said he wanted to show me something. He drove us out to this tiny village an hour from Paris. There was a park there, overgrown and forgotten. And in the middle of it, this old carousel."

"A carousel."

"It had been closed for years, falling apart. But Thomas had somehow found out about it and had it restored. Not completely, just enough to make it functional. New paint on the horses. Lights that worked. Music that played."

Amy's hand had gone to her heart. "Dawn."

"He remembered me talking about carousels. How I used to love them as a kid. How I always picked the same horse, the one that looked like it was about to run away." Dawn's voice caught. "He found a carousel with a horse like that. In France. And he fixed it. For me."

"And then?"

"And then we rode it. Just us, in this abandoned park, spinning around like kids. And when it stopped, he got down on one knee right there on the platform."

"What did he say?"

Dawn closed her eyes. The memory was vivid, the smell of old wood and fresh paint, the tinny carousel music, and Thomas's face lit by the colored lights.

"He said: 'You spent your whole life looking for a way to run. I want to be the reason you stop. Not because you have to, but because you want to. Because wherever we go, whatever we do, we do it together.'"

Amy was crying. "That's the most romantic thing I've ever heard."

"I know. I told him he'd ruined proposals for everyone else."

"What did you say? To the actual question?"

Dawn smiled. "I said yes, obviously. Then I made him ride the carousel three more times because I wasn't ready for the moment to end."

"And now?"

"And now we're getting married in October, after the Arts Collective opens. Small ceremony, just family." Dawn looked around the room, at her parents bickering good-naturedly about ornament placement, at Will patiently following Junior's very specific decorating instructions, and at Thomas explaining the history of glass ornament making to a toddler who was definitely not listening.

"And now I'm home."

Later that evening, after the adults had settled into the comfortable exhaustion that followed successful family gatherings, Dawn stepped out onto the porch.

The night was cold and clear, with snow falling in lazy flurries that caught the light from the Christmas displays. The town was peaceful, families inside, Christmas Eve preparations winding down, the quiet anticipation that came with holidays, traditions, and time set aside for the people who mattered most.

Thomas found her there, as she'd known he would. He wrapped his arms around her from behind, and they stood together, looking out at Holly Falls.

"Thinking about anything in particular?" he asked.

"The wish I made last year. At the beginning of all this."

"The one you never told me about?"

Dawn leaned back against his chest. "A place to land and someone who won't make me stay or go with me if I leave."

"Did it come true?"

She thought about the year they'd had. The flights to New York when Thomas needed her there. The late-night video calls when board meetings ran long. The compromises and adjustments, and the occasional arguments about whose turn it was to fly where. The careful balance they'd struck between his responsibilities and their chosen life, between the world that demanded his attention and the community they'd chosen to serve.

It hadn't been easy, but it had been worth it.

"Yeah," she said. "It did. You're not making me stay, Thomas. You're giving me reasons to want to."

"Good reasons?"

"The best reasons."

He was quiet for a moment. "I have something for you."

"Another Christmas gift? We said no more presents after the barn renovation went over budget."

"Not a present. A question." Thomas turned her around to face him. "How would you feel about spending next Christmas in New York with my mother?"

Dawn blinked. "Your mother wants to meet me?" she asked.

"My mother has been wanting to meet you for six months. I've been trying to figure out the right time to ask." Thomas's smile was uncertain. "She called last week. Said she'd like to host Christmas dinner. Something about 'finally meeting the woman who made my son happy.'"

"And you want to go?"

"I want you to meet her. I want her to meet you." He paused. "I want to introduce you as my fiancée, and I want to know that when we fly back home to Holly Falls two days later, we're coming back to our life, not my temporary retreat from responsibility."

Dawn looked at him, this man who'd learned to wire pinecones, failed spectacularly at making pancakes, and somehow convinced a toddler that the history of glass ornaments was fascinating. Who'd restructured a billion-dollar company around a small-town life because he'd fallen in love with both the town and the woman who'd finally decided to stay there.

"I'd like that," she said.

"Yeah?"

"Yeah. As long as we come home to the barn afterward, attend the Arts Collective opening, and whatever small-town drama Edna and Marv are planning for the spring."

"Deal." Thomas kissed her forehead. "For the record, I think their spring drama involves a garden competition with the Hendersons. Very serious business."

"Obviously. Gardens are serious business in Holly Falls."

"Everything is serious business in Holly Falls. That's what makes it perfect."

Dawn laughed. She pulled her old compass from her pocket, the one Thomas had found in the barn, with *Find your way home* scratched into the brass. The needle swung, then settled, pointing north. Toward the Arts Collective. Toward the life they were building. Toward home.

"I love you," she said.

"I love you too."

"Even when I make you ride carousels in France?"

"Especially then."

She stood on her toes and kissed him on the porch of her childhood home, with snow falling around them and Christmas Eve settling over Holly Falls like a promise.

A year ago, she'd been running from everything that scared her. Now she was engaged to a billionaire, building an arts center, and planning to spend Christmas with his mother in New York.

Life was funny sometimes. The best kind of funny.

"Let's go inside," she said. "Before we actually freeze."

"Agreed."

They turned toward the door. Dawn paused, looking back at the town one more time.

Holly Falls at Christmas. The place she'd run from, run to, and finally—finally—stayed.

"Hey," Thomas said.

"Yeah?"

"Merry Christmas."

She smiled. Took his hand.

"Merry Christmas."

They went inside, closing the door on the cold and stepping into the warmth of family, future, and everything they'd built together.

The wish was fulfilled. The story was complete.

It ended as it should, not with grand gestures or dramatic declarations, but with two people choosing each other, quietly, completely, in the soft light of a Christmas just beginning.

And in Dawn's old bedroom, Harold the Reindeer sat on the pillow, still offering no commentary but somehow looking satisfied with how things had turned out.

Some stories end with running away.

The best ones end with coming home.

Hello!

My name is Judy Powers, and I have been crafting stories for years, but only recently decided to share them with the world. I specialize in sweet romance where love finds a way, and every character is someone you'd want to know.

When I'm not writing, I'm an empty nester living with my husband and three cats. You might also find my husband on the front porch, offering treats to the local squirrels who've learned exactly where to get a snack!

www.ingramcontent.com/pod-product-compliance
Lightning Source LLC
Chambersburg PA
CBHW051430170626
46809CB00006B/2391